Border Lines

Stories of exile and home

Border Lines

Stories of exile and home

EDITED BY KATE PULLINGER

Library of Congress Catalog Card Number: 93–83891

A catalogue record for this book is available from
the British Library on request

These stories are works of fiction. Any resemblance
to actual persons, places or events is purely coincidental.

'Litany for the Homeland' by Janette Turner Hospital was
first published in *Homeland*, ed. George Papaellinas,
published by Allen and Unwin, Sydney, 1991.

First published 1993 by
Serpent's Tail, 4 Blackstock Mews, London N4, and
401 West Broadway #1, New York, NY 10012

Typeset in 10½/13pt Plantin by Servis Filmsetting Ltd,
Manchester
Printed in Finland by Werner Söderström Oy

Contents

The Day Carmen Maura Kissed Me   *Jaime Manrique*   8

Da Costa's Rupununi   *Roy Heath*   20

Wohlstand   *John Saul*   34

Nobody Leaves a Winning Table   *Hooman Majd*   51

Visitor   *Kirsty Gunn*   67

The Lemon Tree   *Brooke Auchincloss-Foreman*   78

Southern Comfort   *Audrey Thomas*   83

La Vie en Rose   *Leena Dhingra*   97

Capitalism   *Joe Ambrose*   119

Paris-Michigan   *Susan Moncur*   127

Litany for the Homeland   *Janette Turner Hospital*   137

Karima   *Aamer Hussein*   153

Bad News   *Lynne Tillman*   166

Like Having God Pay You A Visit   *Josef Skvorecky*   174
translated by Michal Schonberg

Brief Encounters   *Roberta Allen*   185

Nach Unten   *Janice Kulyk Keefer*   190

Troglodytes   *Susan Schmidt*   199

The Dream Shop   *Romesh Gunesekera*   213

About the Authors   218

Introduction

As the century nears its end, it is easy to feel that the world is becoming simultaneously smaller – theoretically the other side of the globe is only twenty-four hours away – and more and more fragmented. Wars, uprisings, famine, nationalism: all over the world people are fleeing, moving, leaving, trying to find somewhere to make a new home. The stories in this anthology are about re-location, whether that may be the painful involuntary removals of political exile or the more prosaic migrations of folks looking for better lives. Often these movements span thousands of miles, occasionally they take place within somewhere we've always called home.

These stories are fictional explorations of the complexities of belonging and identity, the shifting and cross-cutting cultural experience which has become common to many people as we move about on the planet. Many of the contributing writers live outside their country of origin, and those origins are very diverse. From India to Paris, Guyana to Brazil, the Ukraine to Toronto, people move and re-adjust their lives continually, like the changing weather patterns on satellite photographs of the planet. Weathering exile is never as easy as sheltering from the rain, and these stories embrace a huge range of experience, reflecting some of the hardship but also much of the joy of finding somewhere new and making it your home.

Kate Pullinger

The Day Carmen Maura Kissed Me

JAIME MANRIQUE

I was on my way to the Algonquin Hotel to have a drink with my friend Luis whom I hadn't seen in several years. It was 4 p.m. in mid-June, and looking up the vertical canyons of midtown Manhattan, I saw a lead-colored, spooky mist engulfing the tops of the skyscrapers, threatening rain. As I passed Sardi's, my eyes snapped a group composition made of three men, TV cameras, and a woman. Living as I do in Times Square, I've become used to TV crews filming in the neighborhood around the clock. But the reason I slowed down my pace was that there were no curious people hanging around this particular TV crew. The four people were not students, either – they were people my age. I noticed, too, they spoke in Spanish, from Spain. Then, to my utter astonishment, I saw her: *la divina* Carmen Maura, as my friends and I called her. Almodóvar's superstar diva was taping a program with these men outside Sardi's. It's not like I'm not used to seeing movie stars in the flesh. O'Donnell's Bar, downstairs from where I live, rents frequently as a movie set. Just last week, coming home, I ran into Al Pacino filming in the cavernous watering hole. You could say I'm starstruck, though; and I'm the first to admit it was my love of the movies that lured me to America. But after ten years on Eighth Avenue and 43rd Street, I'm a jaded dude.

Carmen Maura, however, was something else. She was my favorite contemporary actress. I looked forward to her roles with the avidity of someone whose unadventurous life needs the vicarious thrills of the movies in order to feel fully alive. I adored her as Tina, the trans-sexual stage actress in *Law of Desire*. But what immortalized her in my pantheon of the divine was that moment in *Women on the Verge* when, putting on a perfectly straight Buster Keaton-face, she orders the girl with the Cubist profile to serve spiked Gazpacho to everyone in her living room. After I saw the movie, I fantasized carrying with me a thermos of Gazpacho to offer a cup to (and put out of circulation) all the boring and obnoxious people I encountered in my humdrum routines.

Carmen stood on the sidewalk, under the restaurant's awning, speaking into a microphone, while the cameraman framed her face and Sardi's sign above her head.

Riveted, I stood to the side of the men and diagonally from the star, forming a triangle. For a moment, I fantasized I was directing the shoot. What's more, I felt jealous and resentful of the technicians working with Carmen. To me, they seemed common, unglamorous, undeserving of existing within range of the star's aura. I stayed there, soaking in her presence, thinking of my friends' reactions when I shared the news with them. Momentarily there was a break in the shooting and, getting brazen, I felt compelled to talk to her. The fact that I was dressed up to meet Luis at the Algonquin helped my confidence. I was wearing what I call my golf shoes, a white jacket, a green Hawaiian shirt and a white baseball cap that says Florida and shows two macaws kissing. Therefore, it was unlikely that Carmen would mistake me for a street bum.

As I took two tentative steps in her direction, I removed my sunglasses so that Carmen could read all the emotions painted on my face. I smiled. Carmen's eyes were so huge, and liquid and fiery, that the rest of the world ceased to exist. For an instant, I felt I existed alone in her tunnel

vision. I saw her tense up, and an expression of bewilder-
ment, unlike any I had seen her affect in the movies, showed
in her face. Carmen exchanged looks with her men, who
became very alert, ready to defend their star from any
danger or awkwardness.

'Carmen,' I popped, in Spanish. 'I love your movies.
You've given me so much happiness and I want to thank
you for it.'

The star's fulltoothed smile took me aback. Her men
smiled too, and went back to loading their camera or
whatever they were doing.

'We're taping a show for Spanish television,' Carmen
said. She was wearing a short white skirt, and a turquoise
silk blouse and red pumps, and her Lulu hair was just like in
Women on the Verge, except a bit longer. Her lips and
fingernails were painted an intense red, and her face was
very powdered. Extremely fine blonde fuzz added a feline
touch to her long, sleek cheeks. 'This is where *Women on the
Verge* received an award,' she was saying as I landed back
on earth.

A momentary silence ensued, and we stood face to face,
inches away from each other. Her poise and her ease and
her friendliness were totally disarming, but suddenly I
couldn't help feeling anxious. I decided to finish the
encounter before I did something silly or made her yawn. It
seemed ridiculous to ask her for an autograph so, as a
goodbye, I babbled, 'You're the greatest actress in the
contemporary cinema.' That somehow wasn't enough, did
not convey the depth of my emotions. So I added, 'You're
the most sublime creature that ever walked the face of the
earth.'

Any reserve she may have had left, melted. Diamond
beams flashed in her coal-black eyes, which were like huge
pearls into which I could read volumes.

'*Ala!*' she exclaimed, which is an expression that means

everything and nothing. Before I realized what was happening, Carmen glided toward me, grabbed my chin and kissed me on the cheek, to the left of my lips.

I bowed, Japanese style (Heaven knows why!) and sprinted down the street. At the corner of Broadway and 44th, I turned around and saw that Carmen and her men had resumed their taping. My heart wanted to burst through my chest. I was out of breath, almost hyperventilating. I felt strangely elated. Aware of the imbecilic smile I must have painted on my face, I put on my sunglasses. Although the DON'T WALK sign was on, I crossed the street. A speeding taxi missed me by half an inch, but I didn't care – at that moment I would have sat smiling on the electric chair. Standing at the island in the middle of Broadway and Seventh Avenue, I had to stop for a moment to recollect where I was going and why.

'Wait till Luis hears about this,' I thought.

My friend Luis is a film-maker and a movie nut; it was our love of the movies that had brought us together. He had been educated in the States, where he graduated in film-making at UCLA. We had met in Bogotá, in the early seventies. I made my living at that time reviewing movies and lecturing about the history of the cinema at the Colombian Cinematheque. Luis, who was wealthy and didn't have to work, published a film magazine and made documentaries. We were leftists (although we both despised the Moscow-oriented Stalinist Colombian left), smoked a lot of Santa Marta Gold, ate pounds of mushrooms, and it wasn't unusual for us to see three and four movies a day. We were the angry young men of the Colombian cinema; we had declared war on the older generation of Colombian film-makers whom we considered utterly mediocre and bourgeois. I'm speaking, in other words, of my youth. Later I moved to Europe and even later to New York where I now made a living as a college professor. Nowadays I'm haunted by the Argentinian refrain: 'In their youth they throw bombs; in their forties, they become firefighters.' Luis, on the other hand, had remained in Colombia where he continued making documentaries and feature films that were distributed in Latin America but had never been released in the States. Slowly, we had drifted apart. He never called me anymore when he was in New York. But this morning, when I heard his voice, the years in between had been obliterated in one blow and I had joyously accepted his invitation to meet for drinks at the Algonquin like we used to do in the old times when we dressed in jackets and ties so we could have a few drinks while we watched the film critics, movie directors and stars that we idolized and who frequented the place at that time.

It began to sprinkle heavily when I was about a couple of hundred yards from the hotel's awning. I broke into a fast sprint in order not to mess up my jacket and shoes.

The last time I had been in the Algonquin had been to meet Luis. I felt like I was walking into a scene of the past. Maybe the crimson carpet was new, but the rest of the place was dark and quaintly plush, as I remembered it. I told the waiter I was meeting a friend for drinks. There were a few people in the vast room. I scanned the faces looking for Luis. The times had changed, indeed: I saw a couple of kids in shorts and T-shirts drinking beer and munching peanuts. But I couldn't find Luis. I was about to ask for a table when a woman waved at me. I waved back as a polite reflex. When she smiled, I recognized her: it was Luis, I mean Luisa, as he was called in drag. I forgot to mention that even though Luis is heterosexual and has lived with a girlfriend for a long time, he is a militant drag artist.

Blushing, I said to the waiter, 'That's my party.'

Luisa offered me her hand, which I judged it would be inappropriate to shake, so I bowed, kissing the long fingers which reminded me of porcelain pencils.

'You look like a Florida tourist in Disneyland,' Luisa said in English, the language in which we communicated in the States. In this regard we were like the 19th-century Russians who spoke French among themselves.

'Guess who I just met,' I said, taking the other chair.

'Let me guess. You have stars in your eyes – the ghost of D.W. Griffith.'

'You're as close as from here to the moon,' I said, noticing the waiter standing between us. We both ordered Classic Cokes and this, too, was a sign of how much we and the times had changed. I told him.

'Was Almodóvar with her?' Luisa asked, reaching for a peanut.

Of course neither Luis nor Luisa would have been thrilled by my encounter. I remembered they both worshipped film directors; whereas for me, the star was everything. I felt disappointed. In my short memory, I had thought running into Carmen Maura was the most fortuitous coincidence that could have happened before meeting my old friend.

I shook my head fully exasperated. 'She was taping a program with some guys for Spanish television.' I desperately wanted to change the subject. Luisa chewed the peanut interminably. There was nothing effeminate about Luis when he was in drag. I can easily spot transvestites because of their theatricality and ultra-feminine gestures. But Luisa behaved like Luis: reserved, parsimonious in gesture, and with exquisite aristocratic elegance. She wore brown alligator boots, a long banana-colored skirt, a wide black snake belt around the small waist, and a long-sleeved blouse that closed at the neck with an 18th-century School of Quito silver brooch. The chestnut mane of hair was long and flowed all the way to her fake bust. It helped that Luis was extremely skinny and that his features were delicate and that he had a marvelously rosy complexion.

His jade colored eyes, framed by profuse pale lashes, were utterly beguiling. Luisa could have been mistaken for a structuralist pre-Columbian expert, or an Amazonian anthropologist, or a lady photo-journalist who photographed ancient cities in Yemen or some place like that. It took me a few seconds to remember the dynamics of our friendship: Luis and Luisa were the passive ones, the listeners who laughed at my jokes. I was their court jester.

Obviously I had gotten out of the Carmen Maura incident all the mileage I was going to get. I was rescued from my predicament by the waiter who set the Cokes down, asked us whether we wanted anything else, and left mortified with our drinking habits.

Instead of asking about our friends in common back in Colombia, I began with the most generalized question I could think of, 'So what's the gossip?'

'I can't go back to Colombia,' Luisa said with a twinge of sadness in her voice. She sipped her Coke to give me time to digest the news. 'I had to get out of there in a hurry. I was in the middle of shooting a movie. Can you imagine the timing of these people!' Luisa reached for her big straw pocketbook and pulled out a small wooden box. It looked like one of those boxes where guava wedges wrapped in banana leaves are packed for export, except that it was painted black. She set the box between our glasses.

'It's a box for *bocadillos*. Is it for me?' I asked.

'No, it's for me. But open it,' she prodded me.

Suddenly the box looked creepy, weirding me out. 'What is it? A bomb?'

Luisa teased my curiosity cruelly, with her characteristic gothic humor. 'You're not even warm. Just open it.'

'No, you open it,' I said, thinking she was about to play one of her nasty jokes on me.

'OK,' Luisa acquiesced, removing the top of the box.

Inside the box there was a crudely made replica of Luisa.

Now I got it: it was supposed to be a small coffin, and something like dried ketchup was generously splashed over the little doll.

'That's real blood,' Luisa said pointing at the red stuff.

'What the fuck is that supposed to mean?' I asked, horrified.

'Have you become such a gringo that you don't know what's going on in Colombia?' Luisa wanted to know.

'I read the papers,' I said, shrugging. 'I know paramilitary groups are killing prominent members of the opposition. Furthermore,' I continued with my recitation to show Luisa I was still a Colombian through and through, 'I know they're killing left-wing sympathizers and outspoken Liberals. I keep in touch,' I said, as if to absolve myself of all guilt. And yet, it just blew my mind to even think that Luisa might have become a leftist. If we had resisted the temptation back in the early seventies when the pressure had been intense, I refused to accept that twenty years later Luisa had finally succumbed to Marxism-Leninism. On the other hand, I had heard of people in Colombia who had become socialists just out of exasperation with the telephone company.

'First they call you. And they say something like, "We saw your wife yesterday in the supermarket. Or, we know at what time your little son comes home from school." That's the first warning. Then they send you a blank telegram. And finally, you receive this little coffin, which means you have forty-eight hours to get the hell out before they pop you,' she explained.

I felt nauseous. 'Do you mind?' I asked, taking the top of the box and covering it. Next I gulped down half of my Coke. I looked around: Kathleen Turner was now seated at the table nearest to us. She was accompanied by an equally famous journalist. In the past, we would have been dizzy at the proximity of these luminaries; we would have sat there eyeing them, imagining their conversation, reviewing what we knew about them.

'But why did they send this . . . thing to you? Have you become a member of the Party?'

'I hope never to sink that low,' Luisa smirked.

'Then why?'

'Those creeps are our moral majority. They hate communists, liberals, non-conformists and homosexuals.'

'But you're no gay.'

'Of course not. But you tell them that. You try to explain to them that I dress in drag because of . . . artistic necessity, just like Duchamps did. And Chaplin.'

'I hear Muammar Qaddafi loves to dress in drag,' I said, realizing immediately how inappropriate my remark was.

Luisa smiled. 'He must do it for religious reasons, or something like that.'

'So what are you going to do?'

'I'm going to Spain for a while. I'll look up Carmen Maura and say hello for you when I'm in Madrid,' he teased me. 'Sylvia will meet me there in a few weeks,' he added, referring to his longtime girlfriend. 'She had to stay behind to wrap up my affairs. Then we'll wait a year or two until the situation blows over. I don't think I could live permanently abroad. Colombia is home for me.'

Becoming defensive, I said, 'But you can't blame me for not living there. It sounds like I would have been one of their first targets, don't you think? I'd rather be a homeless artist than a dead hero.'

Luisa sighed before she took a long sip. 'Tell me about you. Are you happy? What have you been up to all these years?'

'You'll have to wait until I write my autobiography,' I joked. Becoming serious, I thought: How could I make her understand my present life? A life so different, so far removed from all that stuff? She probably could see for herself that New York had become a third world capital, like Bogotá; and America a class society, like Colombia. But how could I explain my new interests nowadays: body-building, a vegetarian diet, abstinence from sex, nicotine and most mood altering substances? How could I explain that my current friends were not into revolution, not into changing the world, but into bioenergetics, rebirthing, Zen, Buddhism, healing groups, Quaker meetings, *santeria*, witchcraft studies, neo-paganism and other New Age phenomena?

We did go on to lighter subjects as we consumed a few Classic Cokes. We gossiped about old acquaintances and friends in common, the Colombian film industry, the despised enemies of the past, and our favorite new movies. We agreed to meet for a farewell movie before Luisa left for Europe.

It was past six o'clock when we left the Algonquin, which by then was abuzz with all kinds of artistic and quasi-artistic people talking deals.

It had stopped raining, and the rain had washed away the layers of dust and papers that had accumulated since the last summer shower. The oppressive mist had lifted, too, and the worst of the dreaded rush hour was over so that although Manhattan was alive with the promise of night's splendors, the atmosphere felt almost relaxed. Or maybe it was just my mood.

At the corner of Avenue of the Americas, we hailed a cab. I kissed Luisa on both cheeks, closed her door and waved goodbye as her taxi disappeared in the uptown direction. I felt rejuvenated. It cheered me to realize that the affection for my friend was intact and that we'd probably go on meeting for many more years. I meandered across town, enjoying the nippy air, and the pinkish glow of the bald sky over the metropolis. The sun must have hovered someplace over the Hudson, but night seemed to be pushing not far

behind it. The lighted buildings and billboards blazed like
a high-tech aurora borealis. As I passed Sardi's, I noticed
its emerald green sign, and mailbox next to which I had
stood watching Carmen, and the lamppost next to it, which
now projected a circular beam of red-gold light under
which I bathed, basting. I was about to continue on my way
when, looking across the street, I spotted Carmen and her
men still shooting their program. I stood still, becoming
aware of the street separating us and the cars streaming by,
and the slick Manhattanites, and the pristine tourists
hanging out in front of the theatres that lined 44th Street.
And none of these people were interested in *my* Carmen. It
was as if on the screen she had been created for all people,
all over the world, but in the streets of Manhattan she was
only visible to my eyes. I also knew that the magic of the
moment when we first met was past; that it would have been
inappropriate to interrupt her now, or to say hello, or to
remind her that just a couple of hours ago she had kissed
me. As if to snap the picture forever, I closed my eyes upon
the scene and then I started walking toward home, without
once looking back.

I crossed Eighth Avenue. As I passed in front of Paradise
Alley, the porno palace next door to O'Donnell's Bar, the
score or so of crack addicts hanging out in front of my place
of residence were no longer hideous to me. This evening I
accepted them as the evil spirits necessary in all fairy tales.
Pity arose in my heart for them. In their dead angry eyes, I
read their hopelessness and suddenly they seemed as
doomed and tragic as the people who were being wiped out
back home. The man and the woman smoking crack in
front of my door moved reluctantly as I opened the door
and leaped over the puddle of piss that the rain had not
washed away. Taking the steps of the stairs two at a time, I
felt happy and sad in the same breath. It was a new
sensation this happy/sad feeling I experienced. It was

sadness for all that was sad in this wide, mysterious world we tread upon; and it was the unreasonable happiness produced by the tinsel gleam of the glamorous dreams that had brought me to America and for which I had had to wait for many years before brief, heart-breaking in their fleetingness, they became real.

Da Costa's Rupununi

ROY HEATH

It was the territory where cattle were more valuable than land, where currency laws were flouted, even by the indolent officials, who welcomed any work to relieve the monotony and changed dollars into cruzeiros assiduously, in spite of regulations which forbade it.

Most people had crossed the river into Brazil at least once, without being required to show a passport. The licensed diamond dealer flew his plane every week to Bõa Vista to sell untaxed stones, trips that were common knowledge, yet aroused no perceptible reaction from the officials. The emergence of a frontier morality had been facilitated by the freedom of movement of the aboriginal Indians who, until the last century, understood nothing about political borders, and for whom the words Brazil and Guyana meant areas where Portuguese and English flourished respectively.

Mr Da Costa, proprietor of the only drinking place in the settlement, was standing in the doorway. He had served his last customer half an hour ago and looked forward to the eight o'clock performance of his Monday night film. News had got around that the ancient projector was working once more and he prayed that the room would be full. The former proprietor had advised him to do exactly as he did, even if the reasons were not immediately apparent, and he came to understand why Monday night was set aside for the film show. After the Saturday dance – also held in his establishment – and the torpor of Sundays, the week was brought to life again by the film show.

'They burnin' the savannah,' the Indian remarked as he brushed past him to sit at a table.

'They burnin' it yes,' he retorted. 'They always burnin' something.'

'It hot, eh?'

'Yes, it hot bad,' Da Costa gave back.

This short conversation over, the client thought it was time to order.

'A shot.'

The proprietor poured a measure of rum.

'Is where you get so much money from?'

'I work, ne,' replied the Indian. 'Is work I work. Is the firs' time I work this year. Me cousin take me 'cross the river. They got a lot a work in Brazil. But . . .'

He hesitated, judging that he had said too much, for the proprietor had not been there long enough to be trusted. Besides, what did one make of a man who had taken down from the wall the picture of Christ on the cross?

'You comin' to the show to-night?' the proprietor asked, now standing behind the counter and making a show of wiping glasses.

'Is wha' you showin'?'

'A cowboy film.'

'I sick o' cattle . . . and vaqueiros,' the Indian said feelingly. 'I give up me job over there 'cause they wouldn' give me a horse without sores. I sick o' cattle an' cattle people.'

The silence that followed was like a penance for the proprietor, who knew he had not yet been accepted by the inhabitants of the settlement.

'You want a job?' he asked after a while. 'On Monday an' *Satyurday* nights. You can work the projector on Monday an' serve at the counter *Satyurday*.'

'You pay good?'

'Yes. An' you can drink as much free liquor as you want while you workin', as long as you don' get drunk. You does speak Macusi?'

'*And* Portuguese,' replied the Indian.

'Good. We does get Brazilians over here on *Satyurday* nights.'

The slight start the Indian gave at this information was not noticed by the proprietor, who suggested that he should teach him how to work the projector at once.

The two men went into the back shop, leaving the counter unattended. Puffs of smoke entering by the doorway and two windows added an edge to the musty-sweet scent of the establishment; and the whirring of a projector from the back shop contrasted with the silence of the savannah. Da Costa recalled how, the day before, boredom and the mid-day heat had driven him out in pursuit of imaginary customers, wearing a wide-brimmed hat and feather-light clothes. His offer of work to the young man was more a guarantee of company than a response to any need for assistance in running his drinking place, since in the peak hours clients were always willing to serve behind the counter. As for the projector, he himself attended to it.

Mr Da Costa was pleased with his prospective employee's aptitude and they agreed that he should start that very evening.

'Naw!' he exclaimed, declining payment for the young man's drink.

They continued talking and the proprietor reflected that his new employee was unusually loquacious for an Indian. He learned that in Brazil more animals than ever were being killed by vampire bats, especially the calves.

'My boss loss all nine calves. Rabies!'

'That's a lot of calves,' the proprietor said with a show of sympathy, but indifferent to the fate of the unknown rancher's cattle.

And while they talked the proprietor became convinced that the Indian wanted to confide in him. The Macusis, notorious for their attachment to the Rupununi savannahs, had relations the length and breadth of the area north of the Kanuku mountains, so he could not imagine why the young man should wish to bare his soul to a stranger. Perhaps he was mistaken. The Indian's habit of suspending his discourse in mid-sentence might be a quirk that indicated no more than a fondness for scratching behind an ear would. Da Costa, in turn, spoke of his past. He had panned for gold in the bush, worked on a timber grant and had backed porknockers, who built him an air strip and sold him their diamonds for a period of two years. His wife and children were in Bartica, where he intended returning when he got this place going. Who knows? He could possibly leave the business in the young man's charge when it began to thrive and when he was sure of him. But the latter reacted in no way to the suggestion and he was reminded that he had never once come across an Indian businessman.

'I know alyou people don' like business. But you can give it a try . . . when I get to know you.'

But the new employee remained stubbornly unresponsive, rejecting the suggestion as firmly by his silence as he would have done by saying 'No.'

'You say Brazilians does come over here a lot?' the Indian asked.

'Yes. On *Satyurday* nights.'

'They does bring guns?'

'They not supposed to,' the proprietor answered. 'Is against the law here.'

'But does they?'

'Some o' them. But they don' use them.'

'Well,' the employee continued, 'You don' need a gun to kill a man.'

'Suppose not ... They in' had a killing round here since nineteen seventy-two. The place dead.'

Both men were unconscious of the irony in the remark and continued their conversation with the same seriousness, the young man with an expression at once distant and alert, the proprietor eagerly pursuing every opening in an effort to cement their acquaintanceship.

'Why they does burn the savannah?' the proprietor asked.

'It does make the grass grow better, they does say. If you ask me is jus' habit.'

The employee wanted to buy another shot of rum, but was afraid that the proprietor might think he was taking advantage.

'I gone,' he said.

'Don' forget, by seven. Come back by seven.'

'I in' got clock. A lil' time after the sun go down.'

'Eh heh.'

Da Costa followed the Indian to the door and watched him walk off in the direction of the mountains where, apart from one thatched house with cassava cakes drying on the roof, there was a great emptiness, relieved only by termite hills and a few stunted trees.

'I might as well shut the place at day-time,' he muttered, knowing full well he would do no such thing, for want of some supplementary occupation.

The Indian had fled Brazil because he had killed a steer belonging to the *capataz* for whom he worked. He and his fellow Macusi vaqueiros had taken sides with a man whose garden place had been trampled down by some of the *capataz*'s wandering cows. In the drawing of lots to decide who would kill an animal the lot fell to him and he lost no time in slitting the throat of a prize steer when all the men were asleep in the *barracão*. Certain that suspicion would fall on one of the Macusi cowhands he fled towards the river, which he crossed the next night, after hiding during the day. The five Macusis who made up the conspiracy gave him all their wages as part of the bargain.

The young man did, indeed, come from Guyana; but he was at home on the other side of the border, where most of the work was. And now he had condemned himself to long periods without employment. Moreover, it was only a matter of time before he was recognized. The news that Brazilians attended the Saturday night dances had alarmed him and he had not yet decided whether he should accept the job of projectionist and barman, welcome as it was. He had made for the thatched house near the proprietor's cinema-drinking place, where a distant relation lived.

That evening he presented himself as agreed, wearing a complete change of clothing. The proprietor greeted him effusively and poured him a cup of milk, which he sipped behind the bar while he watched the viewers taking their seats and hailing one another. The large number of women at the shows never ceased to surprise Da Costa, in whose home circle women hardly ever attended the cinema, and if they did, were invariably chaperoned.

In due course the room was darkened with two lengths of heavy material over the window, an operation which drew applause from the assembly in anticipation of the show that would begin within a few minutes.

'Da Costa!' a voice shouted out. 'Light still comin' in on this side.'

This ritual cry dated back to the time when there used to be a five o'clock show and the thinnest ray of intrusive light was disturbing to some clients. But the proprietor, anxious to please, pretended to adjust the offending curtain with a flourish. Then, placing himself between the screen and the clientele, he proceeded to give a synopsis of the drama which was about to unfold, ending with the remark: 'Is a historical film.'

'Da Costa, shut you mouth!' a male voice thundered in protest. 'Is a cowboy!'

Everything went off well, so that the proprietor, who had opened his shop that morning dreading lack of company and deploring the isolated situation of his establishment, ended up congratulating himself on his good fortune.

'Funny,' he thought. 'I'm Portuguese an' only talk English, but John is Macusi an' does talk fluent Portuguese.'

He and his employee attended to the counter after the show and it did not escape his attention that the clients were pleased to be served so quickly. Many of them took their chairs outside, under the stars, where bats flitted and the barking of foraging animals carried for miles across the empty savannah. If day-time was like an image of a hell from which noise was banished, night was a respite of shadows and faint sounds.

He had always acted like that, on the spur of the moment, and never once had he been let down. Yes, he was prepared to leave the shop in the Macusi's hands tomorrow, with a two thousand dollar float and without anyone to keep an eye on him. Having become wealthy by working hard and making decisions on the spot there was no reason to change his style now. Each Saturday night takings were larger than the last and the Indians, who liked seeing one of their own behind the counter, kept joking with John, often addressing him in the Macusi language.

Were it not for the poor savannah soil he would venture into farming, his true bent, Da Costa told himself, carried away by his financial success. It was all the more unexpected as the former proprietor had warned that he would need a good two years before people began to accept him. Too many fly-by-nights had set up shop and left within a short time, driven away by the savannah silence and the endless horizons. He had given up his mid-day walks, during which he counted the termite hills and coucourite palms. Instead, he listened to the often unintelligible conversations of unemployed Indians assembled under the adjoining shed, who shared the three free bottles of beer to which John was entitled when he was not working. He saw his shop being transformed before his eyes, imagined that the squash vine on the shed and the unidentifiable fruit tree next to it constituted an orchard where birds congregated, filled the dawns with their cantankerous singing, enriched the ground with their *caca*. Strange! That was the only Portuguese word he knew, one less than his father, who understood the word for *die* as well.

The rainy season was haggling with the dry season, as a visitor to his parents' house used to say. Dark clouds came and went. The sun declared its intention of departing for good but reappeared the following day, clothed in all its finery, mocking the watchers for the rains, which would swell the rivers and allow a passage to the Rio Branco and down the Rio Degro to the Amazon itself. Who could deny the pull of this mesmeric landscape of absences, this Hell-Heaven which drew women out on the occasion of film shows and dances and sucked them back again into their lairs? He had not had a single dream in the fifteen months since he arrived, unless he could count his day-time hallucinations as dreams, an endless file of anteaters, flocks of sun-blanched birds, two horsemen with glittering spurs. Tomorrow, the day after tomorrow, early next week at the latest, the rains would come and turn everything upside down.

'I *did* dream, one time, that I see a jeep driving this way, but getting smaller an' smaller as it come close.'

Perhaps that was a hallucination too.

The rain, following flocks of birds southwards to the Kanuku mountains, drove animals to high ground and obliterated the paths. Small streams became torrential rivers within days and in a fortnight joined to form inland lakes that stretched beyond the border.

John's friends, who now kept away except on Mondays and Saturdays when they came for the film show and the dance, congregated in the shed one Tuesday afternoon during a break in the weather. They did not drink alcohol and their whispered conversation had a conspiratorial quality which seemed entirely appropriate to the Rupununi savannahs.

After they dispersed John came over to tell Da Costa about the episode which caused him to flee Brazil. The friends who shared his drinks were Macusi fellow workers at the time. Unwilling to disclose his whereabouts, the *capataz* had dismissed them with a warning not to look for work in Brazil until John was caught. They were all putting up at the house of his distant relation, who insisted only that morning that two of them would have to leave.

'And you want me to put them up, huh?'

'Yes,' John replied.

The proprietor did not answer at once. Relations with these people were never simple. What had he got to do with John's hordes of friends? *He* could not tell one from the other and harbouring them would be like lodging identical twins. At the same time he was conscious of John's contribution to his success, of his invaluable knowledge, which embraced everything about the Rupununi.

'All right. But I can't feed them. And it'll only be for a few weeks. Understand? A *few* weeks.'

He insisted on the word, knowing that John's vagueness with numbers was of a piece with his imperfect grasp of time.

Da Costa now looked back on their first conversation, recalling his willingness to work and his unease in the presence of Brazilians, especially those whose deportment betrayed an involvement with horses.

'You better bring them now so I can show them where they goin' sleep,' Da Costa said.

At the end of May, when the rapids in a number of rivers had disappeared under flood waters, rendering them navigable to large craft, the Brazilians came from as far away as Bõa Vista. Some brought their Indian ladies to the Saturday night dances, armed with liquor bottles encased in basket-work with elliptical handles. The proprietor, unable to satisfy their demand for samba records, regaled them with sad, slow pieces, evocations of a less violent region. They expressed their dismay in unintelligible Portuguese, but laughed when Da Costa played a tango accompanied by a rasping voice from the low dives of Buenos Aires.

And on those nights John wore a felt hat as a disguise, more vigilant now that the lakes had abolished the frontier. He disavowed any knowledge of Portuguese, shrugging his shoulders when addressed by the strangers or seeking the help of any multi-lingual Macusi near at hand.

His companions, on the other hand, remained out of sight on Saturday nights, judging John's service at the bar to be the height of foolhardiness, notwithstanding his disguise. They played cards while listening to the juke-box music, or gazed through a window beyond the tethered horses belonging to guests.

One night the youngest, a youth of nineteen, declared his

intention of dancing. Against his friends' advice, he ventured into the hall, where all the women seemed to be fanning themselves with their hands after a lengthy piece. Two Brazilians stood out among the mixed company, distinguished by their hats. Instinctively the youth looked down and saw that they were wearing boots. The hats alone would have given them away as cattlemen, but their legwear only served to confirm the impression. He went outside by the front door, doubled round towards the room where his companions were concealed and gave them the news at the open window. He thought he recognized one of them as an employee of the *capataz*.

Concerned that John was in danger of being recognized, the youth went back to the front door and waited for an opportunity to attract his attention. But it was several minutes before John noticed him and came over, bearing a tray from which he had served one of the tables ranged against the wall.

'I see him too,' John said. 'I see him when he come in, but I decide to stick it out. How I goin' leave with so much people? I tell you he in' notice me. Is the hat do the trick.'

In truth his appearance had been altered by the felt hat, a piece from the low estate of a dead townsman, as incongruous in the Rupununi as a formal garden or a pair of patent leather shoes. Confident in his ability to elude discovery he returned to his serving, amidst the cigar smoke and reek of perspiring dancers. Contrary to his own expectations he had taken to the job, to the easy intercourse between client and server so unlike his experience as a vaqueiro, which was marked by a rigid distinction in accommodation and eating habits. The *barracão*, with its open sides and thatched roof, was far removed from the *casa* where the *capataz* and his sons dined. Here there was no humiliation of space.

In the declining night clients began to drift away and the

air seemed cooler with a handful of dancers clinging to each other like children in distress. The Brazilian cattlemen were still there, occupying a table in the company of two Indian women in ill-fitting dresses. They were the last to go and walked with the confident gait of men who had not touched a drop of liquor all night. With a wave of the hand they bade the proprietor good night, then separated from the two women at the door.

John set about placing the chairs on the tables after clearing away the glasses.

'Leave the rest till tomorrow,' the proprietor told him.

And before he left the proprietor gave him an envelope containing his wages, which he did not even bother to open.

On his way to his relation's house a drizzle began to fall and John, thrusting his hands in his pockets, lengthened his stride. The incessant, barely perceptible crackling of the earth in the dry season had given way to the eerie stillness of a water-logged flat land. When he reached the wall, about thirty yards from the house, he bent down to take off his leather sandals, but changed his mind. Then, looking up once more, he saw two horsemen emerge from behind the house with the unhurried gait of vaqueiros herding compliant cattle. John glanced behind him in an effort to judge the distance to his workplace. It would be impossible to make it before a galloping horse.

Pretending that the apparition had not unsettled him he walked calmly towards his relation's house, hoping that, should he be challenged, he would successfully deny having ever worked in Brazil. The gap closed inexorably. Then the horses stopped and the men waited for him, they and their mounts stock-still, as though suspended between sky and earth. John called to mind the harsh treatment vaqueiros meted out to recalcitrant cattle on their way to the corrals, the blank indifference of the *capataz*, and shuddered at a thought that he, like the cattle, was on foot and defenceless.

'Night,' he called, as he went by them.

'John?' one of them said.

Not receiving an answer he repeated, 'John? Your name is John?'

'That's not my name,' John answered, acknowledging in his terror that he understood Portuguese.

'I heard somebody call you John to-night,' the other man said.

'I got a different name.'

'You ever worked over the border?' the same man asked.

'Yes. On the cattle barges to Manaus.'

'Not on Rebeiro's farm?'

'No.'

'Let me see your hands.'

John held up his hands for inspection and one of the men bent low over his horse's mane to examine them.

'It's him,' he told his companion without any emotion. 'He's a vaqueiro.'

'I did work over here with cattle for years,' John protested. 'On the Melville farm.'

The man who had inspected his hands burst out laughing and his colleague, the quiet one, spat on the ground, unmoved.

'We're taking you back,' the quiet one said. 'Get on in front.'

John let out a piercing shriek and both horses shied dangerously, giving him time to bolt. A few seconds later he could hear the pounding hooves behind him, like the very heart-beat of the savannahs. As he ran he perceived a vision of his body expanding into nothingness and began to dream the landscape around him, as piamen did on their journey into the spirit world; and on falling, brought down by a blow from behind, there was no pain, only a terrible longing for the earth and Tawailing, his village on the mountain side.

He was found the next morning by Da Costa; but by the time the dispenser arrived he was dead.

'He must've been in a fight,' the dispenser said. 'They've got to do an autopsy.'

The deed had been expiated: for a steer's slit throat a human life.

The proprietor took charge of the arrangements for John's burial. He and his vaqueiro friends dug the grave themselves. The next day the Indians returned to Brazil and took up their old work, in no doubt that John had been killed by the men in spurs.

Da Costa's business thrived so well that he achieved the status which allowed him to carry a gun, almost as of right. One Saturday night when the two companions with spurs came to his dance he brought out his pistol and placed it ostentatiously on the counter; but the gesture was lost on them and they danced and drank as though their hands were clean.

Rather than go back to Bartica, Da Costa enlarged his house and sent for his family, five girls and four boys, who, had they felt capable of protesting, would have remained where they were, for their way of life was challenged by the forbidding Rupununi savannahs.

Wohlstand*

JOHN SAUL

He was thirty-four, and for three years had lived in this country, its northerly climate, this city, this street, with its drone, drone, car after car, the permanent wind whenever he went down the stairway out into the street, the same wind on the balcony, westerly wind which came with the scudding weather and the draught from the four and five storey buildings. Half of these were post-war brick and window; half wash-coloured, mousse-coloured houses, drained pistachio-greens, ghosted pinks, pale sky-blues of houses, in so many details what he saw and experienced still struck him as foreign. At the sudden sound of a groan from the crowd he turned, to the screen behind; Hartmann had missed in front of the goal, and was sunk on his knees with his head in his hands. This, too, commonly happened; where the English player, shrugging, would have run back to face the goal-kick, here there came usually this interlude of grace and a moment of anguish, hands to the head, or eyes screwing shut, face to the heavens. Yet curiously, when he had once joined a game in the park, and side-footed a ball wide of the goal, someone had said to him baldly: *Das war nicht gut*. So baldly that his spontaneous reaction was to find it vaguely amusing: *Das war nicht gut*. But when the player ran off energetically, clods of mud flying up after him, the net effect had been to leave him

*m -(e)s, no pl prosperity

feeling quashed and disheartened. Should he too have wrung, clutched or beaten some part of his body? And why this circus every Saturday among the professionals? Neither reaction could he much fathom. Did this make football too something foreign? And what did it mean, foreign, used as he used it, was it not just a device for labelling, conveniently filing out of the way, something he was too stupid to understand further?

He looked out again, at the grey parking lot opposite, a car moved into a flat funnel of concrete and he waited to see if the red light of the underground lot would turn green; first amber lights twirled and at last it did go green, the car slipped down the ramp and the door closed behind it; out went the lights, so that then he had no more excuse to be out on the balcony; he came in and switched off the TV. He looked at the time and calculated when Kerstin might arrive home, then remembered she had said something about buying paints, and the sauna with Evelyn, or coffee with Evelyn, for which he accredited himself a further hour and a half. He decided to curse Hartmann for not having scored. He often did score. Then having wrapped up in Kerstin's grey scarf, he collected his season ticket for the bus and the U-Bahn, the Wachsmann Home Furnishings catalogue for the new shelves, his residence permit and his wallet, dropped them into a shopping bag, changed out of his soft wool slippers into his black shoes, and went out.

He moved through the cars to cross over the road, deciding not to take the bus but to walk. It was dry out, not too cold, and the way to Wachsmann's would take him down streets with the attraction of not being familiar. He hurried to be beyond the ring road with its lines of cars, into the comparative quiet of Eppendorfer Weg and then down Weidenstieg, over the bridge with the canal. At the same time he sought to shake the football game from his mind, for it alerted him to scrutinize his surroundings to see if

uniformity was, as he feared, all about him. He looked to see
if the street he was in had at least one house coloured
orange-sorbet, one magnolia, the same pale palette of
colours everywhere; to his annoyance he started checking
how many men wore either black shoes or plimsolls (to his
alarm almost all); and finally, his temper fraying, shaken
into wondering if there could be another society so monotone outside of China, he searched (with success, to his
relief) for women who were not both blonde-haired and
wearing black stockings. This nonetheless common,
repeated sight, proved a saving grace of sorts; for having set
out cursing Hartmann he ended by noticing women, leading him back to what concerned him most, that is, himself
and the woman he lived with, Kerstin.

She had overslept; been in a hurry, drunk no coffee, eaten
nothing. He had watched her dress, nervously, with her
back to him. Usually, when she did not oversleep, she
dressed in the bathroom, the door shut. My hair needs
cutting, was her one remark that morning; while he must
have stared at her in the mirror. But briefly; the sight of her
flesh standing up around her shoulder-straps turned him
away. He felt cheated. Why had she become so fat? Had he
really deserved this assault (her defence, she called it); was
he so unworthy she saw fit to repulse him, push him
physically to one side? But they had, in her words, become
unloving strangers under one roof. This was true. Their
one surviving communal practice was to sit on the sofa
together, languishing in front of the television. It was thus
typical that he should shop for them both, on his own; that
while she cooked, he keep out of the kitchen; that despite all
hoo-hah about women's freedom, the new man, they had
found it advisable to divide their domesticity into pro-
vinces (each to their own wishes and abilities: that had been
the clever formulation in happier days).

He kicked an apple which lay by the kerb, and wondered

if Hartmann's team had gone on to win; then realized he had been watching a recording. A cold zone of air made him look up. There at last was a fine house, along the canal; a wooden house, a warm red, like the earth of fields in Essex he fondly remembered. He turned off his route and walked on by the water.

Kerstin watched a Mercedes manoeuvre out of a knot of parked cars; and when, to get clear, it mounted the kerb and drove up behind her, she resolved not to move more quickly or step out of the way. In her head a moronic-sounding Robert mimicked Janis Joplin singing, 'Lord, won't you buy me a Mercedes-Benz'; she could not then recall him having sung for a long time. The car crept slowly; unflustered, she kept her careful pace. Then turned, abruptly, into the short, thick-cobbled Tegetthoff-strasse; at the end of which, lightly irritated the café should have steps upward, she entered the Sweet Georgia Brown.

Inside were one young man, one woman and a student couple; a glance told her Evelyn had not arrived. The woman reminded her of Dunya, an ex-teacher; but was not Dunya. Only the young man looked up. Five years before-hand, for her face was pretty, his look would have lingered (then, to her distaste); now he turned to the window. Preferring to wait for Evelyn in the upper half of the café, where she could better survey the scene, she started thread-ing her way between tables; with immediate regret. Her hip caught a chair which crashed over, and everyone stared; except for the man, whose dismissal of her presence seemed already concluded. She sat down in bright spot-lights under a speaker discharging a soundwall of flailing, gritty guitar sounds. She had not the self-confidence to get up and move. The elephant sits, she thought stoically. The ele-phant tears down the loudspeaker and stomps it to bits.

Turns a café to matchsticks in a matter of seconds. She
sighed, admonishing herself for daydreaming, and picked
up the menu. No it definitely was not Dunya. Dunya,
Dunya Zulim. She had been passionate for the great
painters. Everyone was or was not a great painter. Always
keep the great painters in mind. Imagine yourself por-
trayed by them, it's an invaluable exercise. Look at yourself
Kerstin. With the light on this yellow menu you are a figure
in (here Kerstin strained for what could be appropriate) an
Edward Hopper painting; you know there is one of a
woman in green at a table with just this marble top, a dark
chair like these ones.

She remembered it; looked down at the menu and
concentrated. This was the pose. The marble was ice-cold
to her hand. A stupid game, stupid Dunya; Hopper could
not be so casually transposed through time and space;
Germany was not the United States. What's keeping
Evelyn? What's Robert up to? Was there no waiter? Where
had she seen pictures by Hopper? She had seen some; who
was she with at the time? Hopper Hopper. Her mind flicked
through images of rail tracks and streets and automobiles;
brute, hard light; lonely figures. She imagined more
closely: herself the painting, Kerstin among the svelte dark
chairs. Her large flesh beneath the coat, her still pretty face.
But her gaze was lowered, the features anonymous. Then
came the uneasy Hopper sensation of the voyeur (Hopper
was a man; men looked at women) transmitted by the
sheen, caught by the light, of her dark stockings below the
table; clothing, but in no way disguising, the voluptuous
beauty of her legs.

She spied the waiter; her thoughts skipped. If this
picture were just a still from a film, then the waiter would
come and she could order the whole menu, which, it being a
film, he would have no trouble in bringing. She would
begin with a soup and work her way through to the apple

strudel with vanilla ice cream and cream, then have another
soup and a different toast, camembert on toast with cranberries, *Preiselbeeren* ... She wanted camembert on toast
with cranberries. This would be the moment at which in
real life Robert would interrupt and suggest, if you want
that then go ahead and have something but why not
something *less*, what about this toast Hawaii, and then she
would just have to have camembert on toast with cranberries, she wanted two orders of camembert on toast with
cranberries. The waiter was coming. She peered first past
the bright lights, expecting Evelyn, but saw only a now blue
gloom around the doorway; she asked for a cup of coffee and
two orders of camembert on toast with cranberries. And
please switch the music down, she added sharply.

It was a jolt to catch sight of Robert, from behind,
crossing Bismarckstrasse at the corner of Weidenstieg. She
would like to have seen his face, not knowing she was
observing him; would he have had that self-pitying look she
always now noticed? He crossed, towards the canal.
Finally, finally, he might be busying himself with their
shelves for the living room. What a fuss he'd made, oh
Kersty what an expense, why bother with new shelves, and
what time have I got, oh Kersty, oh Kersty, the same words
which once escaped in elation for their love-making but
now came out so differently, forlorn and wingeing. But she
mustn't turn sentimental; think shelves and don't think
Robert, Robert and I. He walked behind a removal van,
went out of view. She had assured him: he'd be glad once
the shelves stood there, his books and papers neatly sorted.
Two years over a sofa; then who has sat on it every night
since? Two years for everything, she figured; mention a
new bed tomorrow and it would arrive promptly two years
hence. Which mattered little now; she had found the
apartment she wanted, in Eppendorf, a move up in the
world. The contract was concluded and lying in her

drawer; all that remained was to tell Robert and help him out of their flat in good time, get him over the initial shock of her leaving him.

Her coffee came, with a biscuit, which she munched into. She watched her Dunya stand and zip up her jacket. Take your great painters and go, she thought to herself. She didn't much care for the venue. It was Evelyn suggested the Sweet Georgia Brown, calling it lively. She stared at the chair; then at the other chairs. Where was Evelyn? (Not a set, she saw immediately; who could afford a thirty-piece set of café chairs, when so much furniture had been destroyed in the war.) All were the one dark wood but different designs; one was even rather pretty, the seat had holes like a doily pattern, forming the shape of a star. She looked from there to the student's wrist at the next table; the time, three-forty, tallied with hers. She decided she would eat, then if Evelyn had still not arrived she would go.

Along Kaiser-Friedrich-Ufer Robert relaxed in the relative quiet, stopping occasionally to stare at the water. He opened a letter from his father and mother, which, as ever, disclosed virtually nothing. We had drinks with the so-and-sos; Mary's brother has gone into hospital; on Friday Jo somebody's cousin collapsed, almost died; each person was someone he may have met once in thirty-four years. His mother's charity work went on; she nursed his father with his manifold ailments. Little changed but the date, and the names, the chaotic arrays of stamps.

He paused to watch two boys with fishing rods, not believing there could be life in the oily-thick water. They dropped their rods and began larking, racing through the trees on the mudded incline of the bank. He walked on, admiring the red canal house as he passed it, the leafy setting and the charm of the little landing stage.

No one, he reflected, was more un-German than his mother, with her accommodating, appeasing temperament. When small he must have played on her malleability; must have realized early she would yield and give what he wanted. In her saying no the message he'd got was: I'm saying a no but if you keep on at me (in the right ways of course, let me teach you) I could change it to yes.

Keep on at her how, he thought, fixing his gaze on the bicycles in the middle distance coming towards him. He moved clear of the track. When *she* wanted something she had two ploys: make him feel guilty, or make him feel he had failed. (Reason, on which she was not strong, played next to no part.) He doubtlessly employed all three of these in negotiations with Kerstin. But in Kerstin he had chosen someone direct, apparently strong, whom he thought he could better respect. He did not want his mother, but the opposite of his mother; and having found her, it seemed did not want that either.

He reached the spot he had been looking for, across from the little bridge at the end of Heymann Strasse. Next to the children's playgrounds was the grass mound, bricked into the shape of a quadrant, with its plaque saying this is where Nazis (he walked over to check: did it say Nazis?) burned books in nineteen thirty-three. In fact it was not quite as he remembered. There were four plaques, not one. Where books are burned, in the end people are too, wrote the poet Heinrich Heine. The plaque stone was the smooth quiet brown used for tombstones, and though just three years old the next one had been daubed, defaced and scrubbed; words were fading. Here on the 15th of May 1933 books were burned by National Socialists, he deciphered; five years later the synagogues burned.

He asked himself: would he have acquiesced, assented? One evening at Kerstin's parents' Alphons and Marie-Elisabeth had said: what else was there to do? We were very

young then, you know. To Alphons, moreover, came the
boon of work; we didn't know what was happening, said
Marie-Elisabeth. They hadn't a great deal to say. Recently
he had become aware some people had resisted, hiding
Jews and helping them reach safety, throughout the thirties
and into the war; but his stating that in conversation would
(advised Kerstin) have been construed as edging toward a
judgement (whereas he wondered only, what would *he* have
done?). It occurred to him that he had never heard a person
say: given the time over I would have behaved differently;
was this not a natural enough thing to have said? He had,
furthermore, never asked Kerstin this question, what did
she think she would have done; nor heard her talk about this
more than remotely.

He turned away from the mound, suddenly remembering the shelf business, the living room – he might even see a
desk he liked. He retraced his steps, past the empty
playgrounds. On a bench a father sat tending to a pram.
How Kerstin had cherished such a picture of him, with
child. But now, glimpsing this child, he looked to the man,
thinking: there lies the nascent psychoanalyst; there sits,
now hovering, his raw material. Not an experience he
fancied, or intended; let him go quietly with his foibles to
the grave. Meanwhile would this child learn feeling guilty,
feeling failed; and have a Kerstin then to despise him for it?
The other way round (and here he felt himself reaching new
ground), if *he* made *her* feel guilty, she hated it and turned
on him; and if he implied that she had failed, this cast him
immediately in her father's role. Alfons, the loved and
hated figure of authority whose disciplinary sorties, what
Kerstin called his anxiety for *control*, had driven her at
sixteen from the family home.

He felt weary, and sat on the last bench by the canal. It's
become strenuous to think of you, he explained to Kerstin
as their last heart-to-heart ripped apart. He sought a safer,

less exhausting way to think of them; he closed his eyes, opened them. They were rising up a block of government offices in a paternoster (bureaucracy having changed little since the nineteen thirties), about to sign a contract of co-habitation; they were holding files of documents and waiting for the man at the desk with his little green ruler. This man, whom they had caught telling his assistant to stack envelopes alphabetically before taking them to the post box, informed them, in all solemnity, he personified the State. They watched him, now intent on ruling to the end of his line without complications. As he sat back admiring his handiwork, then reached for his beloved merry-go-round of rubber stamps, there was a clapping sound, and wings flapped, as geese rose powerfully from the water of the canal; he watched them go.

He came to the street; pressed the button for the pedestrian walk light; again turned to the shelves. Kerstin would like them unvarnished, with drawers for papers, dividers for the records, and preferably not made of spruce. He had that hopeless, leaden feeling when trying to buy something to her specifications. He pressed and pressed the button. There would be no drawers the right size, parts would incorporate unseemly plastic, the entire range of systems would be made exclusively of spruce; or a crueller, more ironic twist awaited him.

He pressed again. As twos and threes from the Kaifu swimming bath gathered across the street he tried not to look at them as might a man in depression, seeing people in a mass, but noted instead the attractive traits of individuals: a confident smile; a thoughtful, intelligent face; a rich winter tan. Momentarily the street cleared of cars, while the light stayed red; again Robert cursed Hartmann, for acting like everyone else, as nobody moved.

* * *

Kerstin pulled out a chair for Evelyn's bags.

'Well?' said Evelyn, looking for an empty peg on the coatstand.

'I've decided,' said Kerstin. 'I'm leaving next month.'

'Like I thought,' said Evelyn. 'You couldn't go on how you were. And he wouldn't leave you. He's too wishy-washy for that.'

'Robert is not wishy-washy.'

'All right, not my type. Not your type either. You need someone with more get up and go.'

'What an apt phrase Evelyn, as that's what I'll be doing. And why won't you sit down?'

'I've been on the move. Therapist. Shopping. Badminton. Organizing holidays. Sometimes I go round so fast I don't stop easily.'

'Don't talk such rubbish, and sit. Where are you going on holiday to?'

'I want to get something to eat.'

'What's wrong with the waiter? Sit down for God's sake.'

'All right, all right. What are you eating?'

'Camembert. Preiselbeer. I'm an elephant.'

'We're going to Berlin for the weekend. Why don't you come?'

'Here he comes now.'

'I haven't looked at the menu.'

Kerstin turned to the waiter.

'She hasn't looked at the menu.'

'Oh great, Kersty that's just great.'

'He'll walk round later, you'll see,' Kerstin said. 'So who's going to Berlin? And where are you going on holiday to? Surely not the Algarve again?'

'Margaret, Brigitte and me. You don't sound upset.'

Kerstin sipped her coffee.

'I'm all right,' she said. 'Do you mean holidays or Berlin?'

'Berlin,' said Evelyn.

'Which Brigitte?'

'Albrecht.'

'No men?'

'There are men in Berlin. Besides, this is no time for a man. Not for you.'

'I'm so fat Evelyn. I can't get into half my clothes any more. I keep letting out buttons.'

'Take it easy.' Evelyn put a hand on her wrist. 'One thing at a time. How was the school today?'

'Nightmarish. The staff can't agree and the upper echelon is losing patience. Apart from which, the job is awful.'

'It's a dump I can see; I can sympathize. And with Robert brilliantly freelancing all over the place it must be doubly galling.'

'That's got sticky too, of late.'

Evelyn took out her cigarettes.

Kerstin shook her head. 'The nub of the matter is,' she said, 'I learned to rely on him. Then found he doesn't love me.'

'Men.'

'For me it's not so simple.'

Evelyn sat forward to light a cigarette. She blew a long breath of smoke toward the ceiling.

'I can't stay long today. Let's meet again tomorrow.'

'All right,' said Kerstin.

'God, look at that through the window. I swear that wasn't there last time I was here. That on the wall out there. It's been painted. How do people do that without getting caught?'

'Oh yes. Why did I not see it? What is it? Who are they?'

'In the dinghy, that's an Arab. A Palestinian if you ask me. And the one with a machine gun, losing his machine gun and drowning, well he could be a German for all I know. An American. A soldier.'

'Evelyn I'm so weary. Robert has worn me into nothing.'

'But you will recover.'

'I suppose I will.'

'Wait! There's the waiter. I want an Alster Wasser and let's see ... number 17. Would you like something stronger? Cognac?'

'I'm all right. I'm just tired. I'm not going to start crying or something. I'm all right, really.'

'The way you keep saying that makes me think the opposite. Over-reaction suggests the problem lies in your-self and not out there.' She exhaled abruptly. 'God, I'm beginning to sound like my own analyst. You know what she said to me yesterday?'

'Oh God. Don't give me that schluck Evelyn.'

'Schluck? What's schluck?'

'I'm sorry,' Kerstin sighed. 'I mean ... I've got to sort this whole thing out.' She drank down her coffee. 'I'm tired all of a sudden. I think I'll go home. What did your therapist say anyway?'

'She said if you try sharing a burden for too long you end up lapsing into grief yourself.'

'I don't share a burden.'

'Well all right. All right. You're not going to go before I eat are you? Don't you like this place?'

'I'll call you.'

Past the red house again, the boys with their fishing rods, he hurried back down Weidenstieg and at the end caught the light to cross Fruchtallee. He glanced at the tall spire of Christuskirche, islanded in the river of traffic; then has-tened over the far lanes and headed toward the district known as Sternschanze, past TV and hi-fi shops, a Dro-markt, shopfronts with everything from bathroom fittings to cars and pianos. Wachsmann Home Furnishings would be his third attempt at finding shelves in a week. His dread returned. Spruce, it would be in spruce; and when he finally entered and was served by Frau Wachsmann in person, and the sizes fitted specifications, and the drawers were compatible, the wood was unvarnished, and the dividers had no unsightly plastic parts, sure enough the whole system came in solid (said Frau Wachsmann confidently), top-quality, selected spruce.

Outside, the wind swept across a bare, open crossroads. The sky had darkened, and at the end of a red trail of vapour red clouds moved; in another front, further into the horizon, stood long streaky clouds of indigo. While waiting for the lights to change he tied his scarf more tightly. To think Hartmann had to go out playing in this. Every sixth player, he had read in *Der Spiegel*, sat out the match day injured. Otherwise formulated, each player could expect to spend two months of the year injured, so many days in hospital. Hartmann had all this to contend with; plus the threatened sanction of dismissal. When he missed in front of the goal was it not then natural he should get upset and show it?

Das war nicht gut. This meant: don't let's beat about the bush, we'll call things by their names and face whatever ensues. If the word control had no place in his thoughts until his rows with Kerstin this did not mean the idea itself, control, arose with her; his notion of control had perhaps been less rude, more roundabout, never baldly named; but there all the same. Did he want then to control her? Yes; no. He knew what he wanted. He wanted her to behave, without hard lines drawn, in certain, roughly definable ways. Was that too much to want? Was that not what she wanted too? And so what? Should they in all seriousness sit down and draft a contract?

The tailwind from a heavy truck made him step back smartly. He looked round to make sure he was standing somewhere safe. New, unlaid kerbstones trailed in broken

lines in each direction. His eye drawn down each street, the
buildings now lit but cut in silhouettes, he could not help
but notice the gaping holes, filled awkwardly by the brick
and window housing, torn by the Allied bombs. It was a
familiar, ubiquitous sight; he shrugged; and crossed on the
red.

Then came more roadworks, modernizing the lane-
system, and he had to weave a way through the striped
barriers and tapes, step between the stacks of paving slabs,
huts and compressors, the clutch of cars. He would go as far
as Sternschanze and then take the bus back home. Sternschanze was a haven where he felt at ease. He saw it as the
habitat of the city's last, disappearing demimonde; dirty,
unkempt, in places painted garish colours, decorated with
outlandish murals on the walls.

It began here, the Café Kiesling; next door came the Café
Kepce. Through a window, an enticing pool of yellow light
fell on a billiard table. He passed a Latin voice; French;
Turkish; shops of curiosities, bargains; food being cooked
in basements: was this foreign too, another brand of
foreign? And the poetic vistas which beckoned here and
there between the buildings, with glimpses of a harmo-
niously laid out settlement, trees, gardens, were they also
not part of living in this city?

As he turned back for the bus a mural of an Arab soldier
in a dinghy took his attention. A face in a green helmet
decalled with the stars and stripes, tossing away his gun,
was sinking in the waves. Underneath it said: What was the
Marshall Plan? And the answer came: I don't know. Now
sensitized, he saw graffiti everywhere. Think Global, one
insisted. Another, in English: The Arab world is coming!
But first, brothers, the US-Europe trade war calls.

He saw a likely desk underneath a pile of bric-a-brac, but
decided it was not the one. He fastened his top coat button.
There was the wind again; above the street, an express train

roared by. In the distance several people waited at the bus
shelter (a sign a bus was coming shortly), and he ran toward
them. The seats, as usual, were taken with bags; every
person stood; he read the timetable over someone's
shoulder. A bus would arrive in one minute; it would take
him home in seven. Already another phase of the day
seemed ended. He felt tired.

He stepped forward to meet the bus, got on the last and
sat, tense, near the back, spending the journey staring up
the ribbing of the floor, towards the driver's area.

Robert slipped his key back in his pocket, calling her. He
unwound his scarf, hung up his coat.

'Kerstin?'

'Hello Robert.'

'I thought I heard you. Are you in the living room or in
your room?' He changed from his black shoes into his
slippers.

'I'm in here.'

Kerstin was sitting at her desk looking at old photographs. Robert sat on the bed. She went on looking at the
photographs.

'How was the school meeting?'

'Terrible.'

'Were you in the sauna with Evelyn? Did you go to the
Finnish one?'

'There was no time.'

'What are you doing with those pictures?'

'Oh Robert,' Kerstin sighed and sat back. 'I'm doing
what I'm doing.'

She held a strip of brown negatives up to the light.

'There was no time for the sauna. And it wasn't a definite
arrangement. We just sat in a café and talked.'

'Where?'

'Where? The Sweet what is it. The corner of Tegetthoff-
strasse and Bismarckstrasse.'

'Ah yes, I think I know.'

The amber lights of the underground parking lot
flashed; he looked out of the window. 'Aren't you going to
ask if I triumphed with the shelves?'

'Did you?'

The light turned green; a Mercedes slipped down inside.

'No. Kersty.'

'I see. Robert.'

'What are you sorting? Show me that picture there – that
one,' said Robert moving forward.

'It's yours,' said Kerstin calmly. 'These ones are yours.'

Nobody Leaves a Winning Table

HOOMAN MAJD

'It's just a few more miles to Barstow,' said Parviz from the back seat. 'You can go to the bathroom at the Denny's. Or is the Denny's in Baker?'

'I don't care,' said Dariush. 'Just stop at the first gas station.'

'I think it's in Barstow,' said Bahman, the driver of the car. 'We can have coffee there, too.'

'You can have coffee later, but if you don't stop in five minutes I'll piss in your car.'

It was 2 a.m. when Bahman pulled into the parking lot of the Denny's in Barstow, just off the I-15 in the California desert. Dariush jumped out of the car and ran inside, while Bahman and Parviz slowly made their way to the entrance. Bahman held the door open for Parviz.

'Should we sit at the counter?' he asked, as they stepped inside.

'Sure,' said Parviz. 'It's faster.'

Dariush joined them at the counter a few minutes later. A cup of hot coffee was waiting for him. He took a sip, and took out a pack of Dunhills.

'Let me have one,' said Parviz.

'What time do you think we'll be in Vegas?' asked Dariush, taking a cigarette and throwing the pack to Parviz.

'We should be there by five,' answered Bahman. He took out his Winstons and lit one.

'Pity my Jag is in the shop,' said Dariush. 'I can drive L.A. to Vegas in four hours.'

'Your Jag is always in the shop,' said Parviz.

'Why don't you sell that piece of shit?' said Bahman. 'Get something reliable. Like a German car.'

'You don't understand,' said Dariush, taking another sip of coffee. 'A Jag is like a beautiful woman: take care of it, treat it well, and it'll respond beautifully.'

Parviz laughed. 'What use is a beautiful woman,' he said, 'if she's always on her fucking period?'

'Come on,' said Bahman. 'Let's get out of here.' He took a dollar bill from his pocket and dropped it on the counter. Parviz grabbed the check and stood up. 'We have to pay at the front,' he said. 'Right?'

They were back on the highway five minutes later. Bahman was once again behind the wheel, but Dariush had changed places with Parviz.

'Let's all sit at the same table,' he said. 'Maybe we should even partner.'

'I'm not playing blackjack,' said Bahman. 'Craps. It's the only decent game in the casinos.'

'I don't understand craps,' said Parviz. 'A bunch of redneck Americans yelling and screaming, what kind of game is that?'

'You should learn it,' said Bahman. 'It's a good game, and the odds are better than at blackjack.'

'I like our own "21",' said Dariush. 'I've always played it and I've always liked it.'

'And you've always lost at it,' said Bahman.

'That's not true, I always get way ahead. It's just that I sometimes run into bad luck at the end.'

'I don't know,' said Parviz. 'It seems to me the dealers are out to get you. Whenever you're ahead, a new one shows up and starts getting twenties and twenty-ones all the time. I'm sure they cheat.'

'Nonsense,' said Bahman. 'Blackjack is just a loser's game. I used to lose my rent money at the Playboy Club in London, every damn month.'

'You seem to lose at craps, too.'

'Not always,' said Bahman. 'I think we should check in to a hotel when we get to Vegas,' he added. 'We can sleep first and gamble in the morning. How does that sound?'

'It sounds stupid to me,' said Parviz. 'Let's win some money first and then get a room.'

'If we go straight to the casino, we're not going to leave the tables until we have to go back to L.A. You know that.'

'Let's just see how we feel when we get there,' said Dariush. 'Can't you drive faster, Bahman?'

'I don't want another ticket. And I'm doing seventy, so shut up.'

'Well I'm going to sleep back here for a while,' said Dariush. 'If you get tired, wake me up and I'll drive.'

'I'll drive when he gets tired,' said Parviz. 'I'm wide awake.'

Parviz could see the city lights. He was driving now; Bahman and Dariush were both asleep, snoring. He reached across and shook Bahman's shoulder. 'Bahman,' he said. 'Bahman! Wake up. We're there.'

Bahman opened his eyes. 'Vegas?' he asked.

'Areh. Where are we going first?'

Bahman turned around to look at Dariush. 'He's still asleep,' he said.

'Wake him up,' said Parviz.

'Dariush! Boland-sho,' said Bahman.

'Huh?'

'We're in Vegas,' said Parviz. 'Come on, wake up.'

'OK, OK,' said Dariush, sitting up. He rubbed his eyes. 'Where are we going?' he asked.

'Let's go downtown,' said Bahman.

'Are we getting a room?'

'I think we should.'

'Then let's go to Caesar's,' said Dariush. 'It's much better than downtown.'

'It's a lot more expensive too,' said Parviz. 'Let's go to the Horseshoe; the rooms are cheap and the casino's the best in town.'

'I think Dariush is right,' said Bahman. 'Let's get a room at Caesar's, and then go and play downtown.'

'So it's settled,' said Dariush. 'We'll go to Caesar's.'

'Fine,' said Parviz. 'What are you doing?' he asked Bahman, who was searching inside the glovebox.

'I want to put some music on.'

'Forget it. We're almost there.'

'Here,' said Bahman. 'How about Steve Winwood?' He inserted a cassette into the tape deck and turned the volume up.

They walked in together, the three of them, and made their way through the casino toward the reception desk. At Caesar's Palace, as in most other casinos, one has to pass by the gaming tables in order to reach the lobby. Parviz stopped suddenly at one of the blackjack tables. 'I'm going to play a few hands,' he announced, 'while you guys go and check in.'

Dariush looked at Bahman. 'I'll play too,' he said. 'Why don't you check in for us?'

'No,' said Bahman. 'Come on, let's go and check in. Shit,' he added, 'we've got all day to gamble.'

'Just half an hour,' said Parviz. 'Why don't you play too? I promise, we'll go in half an hour.' He sat down and took out a fifty-dollar bill. 'Change please,' he said to the dealer. Dariush sat next to him and changed a hundred. Bahman watched over their shoulders. They placed ten-dollar bets and were dealt two cards each. Parviz had a twenty; Dariush a thirteen. The dealer showed a nine. Dariush drew another card; an eight. He looked at Parviz and smiled. The dealer showed his hole card; another nine, and quickly paid the winners. Parviz turned to Bahman who stood directly behind him. 'This is a good table,' he said. 'I can feel it. Aren't you going to play?'

'No, I'll go to a craps table. I'll be back in half an hour.'

An hour went by before Bahman returned. He strolled up to the blackjack table, hands in his pockets. He stood behind Parviz again, tapping him on the shoulder. Parviz turned and looked up.

'How did you go?' he asked.

'I lost,' said Bahman.

'How much?' asked Dariush, without taking his eyes off the table.

'About two hundred. What about you?'

'We're ahead,' said Parviz. 'Sit down, this is a good table.'

'How much have you won?'

'I'm up three hundred.'

'I've won about six hundred,' said Dariush. 'Sit down, you'll win your money back.'

'Ok,' said Bahman, pulling a chair out. 'I'll play for a while; maybe my luck will change.' He took out a hundred-dollar bill and placed it in the small circle in front of him. 'Money plays,' he said to the dealer.

'Money plays,' echoed the dealer, looking over his shoulder at the pit boss. The pit boss nodded, and the dealer started to deal the cards. Bahman drew a fifteen; he looked at Parviz nervously.

'Don't draw,' said Parviz. 'The dealer will bust.' He was right. The dealer drew a king to his twelve, and paid everyone at the table. 'Didi-goftam?' said Parviz, grinning. 'I told you it's a hot table.'

'I suppose so,' said Bahman. He took his winnings and placed a green twenty-five dollar chip in the circle.

Hours later, the three were still at the same blackjack table. Bahman closed his eyes and rubbed his neck during a shuffle break. Dariush and Parviz both lit cigarettes. 'Let me have one too,' said Bahman. 'I'm out.' Dariush pushed the pack toward him. Bahman took a cigarette, put it between his lips, and struck a match. 'What time is it?' he asked, as he held the match to the cigarette.

Dariush flicked his ashes into an ashtray and looked at his Rolex.

'Six,' he said. 'In the afternoon, I guess.'

'God! We've been sitting here all day!'

'Don't complain,' said Parviz. 'We've been winning, haven't we?'

'Yeah, we're ahead,' said Bahman. 'But I think we should take a break.'

'You're fucking crazy. Nobody leaves a winning table.'

'It'll be here when we get back.'

'It's never the same,' said Dariush. 'You can leave if you want to; I'm staying.'

Bahman was quiet for a while, hungry and exhausted, but he couldn't bring himself to leave the table. Hours later, after many ups and downs, all three began to lose steadily. The losses became heavier as they repeatedly doubled, and then re-doubled their bets.

'Come on,' said Bahman at one point. 'Let's leave before we lose all our money. This table is ice cold.'

'It'll change,' said Parviz. 'It's been good all day and all night; it'll get hot again, trust me.'

'You said we'd leave as soon as we'd start to lose. We're losing.'

'We've been on cold streaks before,' said Dariush. 'Don't worry.'

'Well I'm leaving,' said Bahman, looking at the cards he'd just been dealt. 'Fucking fifteen! What am I supposed to do with cards like these?' He played the hand, lost, and pushed his chair back. He picked up his chips from the table. 'I'll be at the crap tables,' he said, turning to leave.

Bahman was leaning on a crap table, playing with the chips in his hands, a cigarette dangling from his lips. He watched the action closely and didn't notice Parviz and Dariush standing behind him.

'Aay, Bahman!'

He turned around.

'How much money do you have?'

Bahman held up his red chips. 'Not much,' he said. 'Why? Did you guys lose all your money?'

'Areh,' said Parviz. 'Give me one of your chips.'

'I suppose you want one too,' said Bahman, giving them one chip each. He put the rest on the field, and watched the roll. It was a seven; he lost. He turned around again, but Parviz and Dariush were already gone. He left the table and walked through the casino, looking for them. He finally found them, at a blackjack table in the second casino room on the other side of the hotel.

'Are you winning?' he asked.

'No,' said Parviz. 'This is it, last hand.'

'What about you?' asked Dariush.

'I lost.' Bahman watched them lose the final hand. 'Let's go home,' he said.

'I'm starving,' said Dariush. 'Let's eat breakfast before we go.'

'We don't have any money,' said Parviz, pushing his chair back and standing up.

'We can use my credit card,' said Dariush, also standing.
'But don't even ask, Parviz. I'm not getting a cash advance.'

There was very little early morning traffic on the highway
to Los Angeles. Bahman was driving, Parviz sat next to him
and Dariush was in the back seat. After a long period of
silence, Bahman took out a cigarette from his pocket and
pressed the car lighter.

'It's a beautiful desert, isn't it?' he said.

'Let me have one of those,' said Parviz.

Bahman handed him the pack. 'I mean, it doesn't compare to Iran, but it's still beautiful.' He lit his cigarette and
passed the lighter to Parviz. He rolled down his window a
fraction. 'Why don't you put some music on?' he said.

'What do you have?'

'Look in the glovebox.'

Parviz opened the glovebox and searched through the
tapes. He picked one and closed the glovebox.

'What are you putting on?'

'Shahidi. *Negaheh Garmeh-tow*.'

'Perfect,' said Dariush. 'Depressing music for the
depressed.'

'Go to sleep if you don't like it,' said Parviz.

'*Kir-to-dahanet*,' said Dariush.

'Come on guys,' said Bahman. 'Just play the tape,
Parviz.'

Dariush stared out of the window. 'Don't you get
depressed?' he said. 'Thinking about Iran, I mean.'

'Of course,' said Bahman. 'Especially listening to Shahidi. But there's no music like it in the world.'

'It's hard to believe Shahidi was a SAVAKI,' said Parviz.
'With a voice like that.'

'He wasn't a torturer, for God's sake,' said Dariush.

'Lots of people worked for SAVAK; some of them were good people.'

'I can't believe you just said that!' said Bahman. 'I mean I like Shahidi's music, but let's face it, he was a bastard.'

'Don't be ridiculous. He's decent enough.'

'Decent? He was an informer! How can an informer be decent?' Bahman threw his cigarette out the window.

'Wait a minute,' said Parviz. 'Dariush is right. Some people were forced to work for SAVAK, they had no choice. Shahidi was one of them.'

'That's no excuse.'

'Oh come on,' said Dariush. 'The SAVAK was better than Khomeini's thugs.'

'Why do you always have to compare the Shah's regime to Khomeini's?' asked Bahman. 'So you can justify the Shah? Both systems are bad, and you know it.'

'No I don't know it. And what was wrong with the Shah, anyway? What did he ever do to you? You were happy, don't deny it.'

'I was stupid,' said Bahman. 'I was also happy when Khomeini took over, just like forty million other Iranians.'

'You can't deny that the Shah was better, Bahman,' said Parviz. 'We were wrong about Khomeini.'

'Maybe we were,' said Bahman. 'But that's not the point. Being wrong about Khomeini doesn't make the Shah good.'

'I wasn't wrong about Khomeini,' said Dariush.

'No, you weren't,' said Parviz.

'It doesn't matter,' said Bahman. 'We needed a revolution, and Khomeini was there. We need another revolution now.'

'And I suppose your Mr Rajavi will lead it?'

'He's not my Mr Rajavi: I'm not a Mujahed. You know that, Dariush.'

'Well you sympathize with them.'

'I admire them,' said Bahman. 'They've got guts, but I don't particularly like their philosophy.'

'If the Mujahed'din take over in Iran, they'll be just as bad as Khomeini.' Dariush paused to light a cigarette. 'Iran needs the monarchy.'

'Iran doesn't need the monarchy, and it doesn't want the monarchy,' said Bahman. 'If Pahlavi ever takes power, there'll be another quick revolution. Iranians don't want another fascist.'

'What do you mean "fascist"?' said Parviz. 'Pahlavi's no fascist. With him there'd be a lot more freedom than there is now.'

'And you'd have your old life back, Bahman,' said Dariush. 'That wouldn't be so bad, would it?'

'Well Pahlavi isn't going to rule Iran, and if he ever does, I'm not going back.'

'You're crazy,' said Dariush.

'I'm not. I don't want to go back to see the same old system. I don't particularly miss the corruption, you know.'

'So you'll never go back,' said Parviz. 'There's always going to be some corruption. It's a fact of life.'

'There doesn't have to be. In a true democracy, there won't be any corruption.'

'What's this "corruption" business?' said Dariush. 'You're too American, Bahman. And democracy? So where's your leader?'

'That's the problem: all our leaders are fascists in one form or another. But eventually there'll be a democracy, because that's what the people want.'

'Be realistic,' said Parviz. 'Iranians don't want democracy, they want a strong ruler. Besides, you have forty million illiterate, stupid people to govern. Democracy won't work, because you have to control them. You have to tell them what to do, what to think.'

'They don't even know what's good for them,' Dariush added.

'Don't be ridiculous! Iranians aren't stupid and they do know what is good for them. They knew they didn't want the Shah.'

'You've made my point,' said Dariush. 'They didn't know how good the Shah was for them. The Shah's problem was that he became weak, and Iranians hate a weak leader. They have to be in awe of their ruler.'

'We didn't get rid of the Shah because he was weak,' said Bahman. 'We got rid of him because he was a dictator. Don't you understand that?'

'You're wrong,' said Parviz. 'No one cared about the political system until he showed his weakness. Then the vultures descended.'

'People in your circles didn't care, but the vast majority of Iranians hated the Shah. Don't be so naive.'

'They hated the Shah when they were told to,' said Dariush. 'The mullahs persuaded them.'

'And someone has to persuade them to hate Khomeini,' said Parviz.

'When that happens, they'll want the new Shah,' said Dariush.

'Why?' asked Bahman. 'Why does it have to be the Shah for Iran? Do you think Iranians can't handle democracy?'

'You think you can have a "little America" in Iran?' said Dariush. 'It won't work; Iran will just become another Lebanon. The lower classes aren't sophisticated enough. Two thousand years of monarchy worked just fine: so will another two thousand years.'

'It didn't work. If the CIA hadn't kept the Shah in power, he would have been gone in '53. People knew then that the monarchy was useless.'

'Yes,' said Parviz. 'But you don't really think that Mosadeq would have been good for Iran?'

'Better than the Shah. Maybe we wouldn't have needed a revolution, maybe we would have had a democracy by now.'

'Who's being naive now?' said Dariush. 'If Mosadeq had stayed, Iran would be communist.'

'I don't believe that . . .'

'In fact,' Dariush interrupted. 'In fact, getting rid of Mosadeq was the only good thing the Americans ever did in Iran. If a Republican had been president in 1979, the Shah would still be in Tehran. And so would we.'

'*Kos-nagoo*,' said Bahman. 'You don't think Iranians have changed since '53? If America had interfered with the revolution, they would have had another Vietnam on their hands.'

'Oh come on,' said Parviz. 'All Carter had to do was tell the Shah to use some force, and he would have. He was waiting for the "green light" which he never saw. Carter, the *madar-gendeh*, screwed us more than Khomeini or the Shah.'

'Areh,' said Dariush. 'Carter wanted Khomeini in Iran. It was an American plan to begin with. It's obvious: they wanted to show the Middle East that they still had power. So they could scare them into doing whatever Carter wanted, particularly regarding Israel. Democrats have always loved Israel.'

'You don't still believe that crap, do you? Khomeini hasn't exactly been good for America, has he?'

'He was good for the oil companies,' said Parviz. 'Everybody knows that America orchestrated the revolution,' he added.

Bahman laughed out loud. 'You and your conspiracy theories,' he said. 'What about the hostages? I suppose America orchestrated that, too!'

'Maybe, maybe not. Who knows what goes on behind the scenes?'

'But Carter lost the presidency because of the hostages! Why would he have been behind it?' Bahman took out his cigarettes and offered one to Parviz, who accepted.

'Maybe it was the CIA.' Parviz struck a match and lit Bahman's cigarette, then his own. 'Or maybe the Republicans. Who knows?'

'Yeah, right,' said Bahman, blowing out a stream of smoke. 'Maybe we should ask Deep Throat.'

'Come on, Bahman,' said Parviz. 'You know what I mean: revolutions don't happen unless someone wants them to, like the Americans or the Russians.'

Bahman flicked his ashes into the ashtray. 'Then why don't you think it was the Russians behind our revolution?' he said.

'Because they're smarter than the Americans,' replied Dariush. 'The Russians wouldn't have chosen Khomeini anyway; he's too anti-communist. And they would have bumped him off as soon as he stopped working in their interest.'

'The Russians and the Americans probably got together on the whole thing,' said Parviz. 'Don't forget Afghanistan.'

'What did that have to do with Iran?'

'There, you see,' said Dariush. 'It's not obvious, but I guarantee you there was some connection. And Nicaragua. That happened the same year.'

'What kind of *ahmaghaneh* answer is that?'

'I don't know about Afghanistan or Nicaragua,' said Parviz. 'But I'm sure the superpowers knew about our revolution way before we did.'

'I have to piss,' said Dariush suddenly.

'I'll stop at the next gas station,' said Bahman.

'I can't wait. Stop the car, I'll piss on the side of the road.'

'All of a sudden you have to piss. You can wait a few more minutes; I don't want you pissing on the highway.'

'What's the big deal? This is a desert, for God's sake! You pissed in the desert, in Iran. Remember?'

'Yes, yes. I remember.' Bahman slammed on the brakes and came to a stop on the shoulder. He turned around and looked at Dariush. 'Go ahead,' he said. 'Piss.'

'I want to change the music,' said Parviz. 'This is too depressing.'

'Put on the Marzieh tape.'

Parviz changed the cassettes while Dariush stood outside, facing the car and relieving himself.

'This is great, isn't it?' said Bahman. 'Turn up the volume.' Dariush jumped back into the car. 'Do you want me to drive?' he asked. 'I'm not tired.'

'No, it's OK.' Bahman put the car in gear and accelerated.

'Marzieh,' said Dariush. 'Where is she these days?'

'In Iran,' said Bahman.

'I think she was here for a while,' said Parviz. 'She didn't like it.'

'I don't blame her, but I wonder how she can survive in Iran.'

'She's retired,' said Bahman. 'She doesn't sing.'

'What a waste.' Dariush lit another cigarette. 'She should come here and record some new songs,' he said, exhaling.

'Yeah. There isn't any good new Iranian music, it's all that koony disco shit.'

'Everything went downhill after the revolution,' said Parviz. 'Including music.'

'Khomeini has shit on all artists,' said Dariush. 'If there hadn't been a revolution, we'd still have good music.'

'Not necessarily,' said Bahman. 'Don't forget that the artists all supported Khomeini. Which means they weren't particularly happy under the Shah.'

'Aay baba! Just shut up, Bahman.'

'But why can't you understand that even if we accept that

the Shah's system was better, it doesn't follow that we shouldn't have had a revolution. If things are bad, you change them. If they get worse, you change them again, but you don't go backwards.'

'I've said it a hundred times, and I'll say it again.' Dariush shifted in his seat, stretching his legs as far as he could. 'Monarchy is the only system for Iran.'

'Maybe Bakhtiar is the answer,' Parviz interjected.

'Never!' Bahman and Dariush said it together. 'Bakhtiar is just the Shah all over again,' said Bahman.

'He's a weakling,' said Dariush.

'What we need is a democratic leader.'

'Stop dreaming, Bahman. There's no one who fits your definition of democratic.' Parviz turned to Dariush. 'Is there?' he asked.

'The trouble is that no one really cares,' said Bahman. 'We're too comfortable in our exile: none of us is really willing to lift a finger for Iran.'

'It's too difficult to get involved,' said Parviz.

'I just want my old life back.' Dariush shifted once again and rolled down his window half way. 'It would be good for me and good for Iran,' he added, throwing his cigarette out. He rolled the window back up. 'Be honest, Bahman,' he continued. 'Wouldn't you really prefer to have the old Iran back?'

'No, I wouldn't. When I think about it now, there were a lot of things I hated about it then.'

'Oh come on,' said Parviz. 'You never complained. And think about all the great times we used to have, in Damavand, at the Caspian. We had money and we could do whatever we wanted.'

'And we had the respect of the entire world. We could travel anywhere, without a visa. Look at us now: prisoners in America. And we're expected to love it.'

'You don't know what you're talking about, Dariush,'

said Bahman. 'We're not prisoners here, and America isn't such a bad place to be. We could be worse off.'

'Areh,' said Parviz. 'That's true. But don't worry guys, we'll all be back in Iran someday.'

'Sure,' mumbled Dariush, sinking in his seat. He stretched his legs out once again. 'I'm tired,' he said. 'I think I'm going to sleep for a while.'

'I'm tired too.' Bahman looked at Parviz. 'Can you drive?' he asked him.

'Areh, pull over.'

Bahman stopped the car on the shoulder and changed places with Parviz. 'I'm changing the music,' he said, as they drove off.

'Fine.'

Bahman took out the Marzieh tape, and inserted the Shahidi cassette back into the player. He leaned back and closed his eyes. He was dreaming, and then he fell asleep.

Visitor

KIRSTY GUNN

The dark house smelled of stomachs. Or maybe it was brains. But always it was the smell of offal cooking, always offal, that was nothing new. You remember, those soft transparent pieces bought cheap at the butcher's and left lying in pots of boiling water until they were cooked through and stinking. Their shiny sides gleamed from the plate, white crescents in pools of pale gravy, soft pinks for lips and tongues.

That was the first thing, the smell of that dark house. Nothing seemed to have changed at all during the years away. Same closed-in house, same shameful smell. The green silk curtains at the window were pulled across the daylight, shading the sofas and tables and hump-back chairs that crowded in the corners of the room. And outside, walking around in the garden, all the bushes and vegetables and huge bright flowers were just as I'd left them, arranged in plots but sprouting goblin arms of weeds from too much growing.

If you'd asked, I couldn't have said why I'd gone back at all. To that light so strong it stung your eyes and turned the grass into needles. I wasn't there for a birthplace. Or for memories. People return to a place to see if they've left anything behind, they don't bring their accessories with them.

But oh, how I was there with my little bag of outfits. I was wearing ripped jeans and a lipstick the colour of fire engines but the minute I stepped off the plane I felt the thin unprotective nature of my coatings. What was the use of any of it here? The bag containing my London things, the frocks and jackets and twinkling earrings, the special case for shampoo and creams . . . What use? When the light and heat and all the years roared up to meet me?

Tripping foolishly across the tarmac in expensive shoes, I thought: This is it, the old place. This is it, had you forgotten? The blue sky was bearing down and all around the green hills rose and sang. Sun struck off the edges of things, off concrete, off aluminium, and in the long taxi ride to my aunt's dark house the plastic on the car seats burned.

'Here for long?'

The cab driver chewed on a cigarette end like it was gum, the back of his neck seemed contented.

'Just two weeks.'

'Yeah? Long way to come for fourteen days . . .'

Two weeks was the time I'd given my boss at work, just two weeks. A short trip back, to check everything was OK. I owed it to Aunt Eila because she was old. It was the only time I'd ever taken a break from the job and she might not see me again.

'Just a visit,' I told the driver, and through the rips in the denim I could feel my skin.

My boss at work is a certain kind of man. Hires all the waitresses because he thinks he might sleep with them. Thinks he's Daddy, thinks we love him and honour and obey. I've held down the job for three years now, the tips are nice. Always, you're behaving: The right smile at the right time, the confidential play of fingertips to prove everything's OK.

'I promise after two weeks I'll be back and it'll be like I never left.'

'You promise you promise?'

I let my hands move amongst his in a way that could make him think one day I would be his lover.

'Don't tell me you can't manage,' I said. 'Baby. It's only fourteen days.'

He put his arms around my shoulders, he was smiling. The lunchtime shift had ended and the cheques had been thick. He was, after all, a glamorous kind of man.

'As long as you come back then,' he said. 'As long as you don't stay there, take up your roots again, some thing . . .'

I put my face in his neck, kissed him there on his little pulse.

'Just as long as you come home to me, darling,' he said.

Aunt Eila was still old and strong when I saw her again. Her letters had made it seem that she was nearly dying, with her friends boxed up and buried, and the garden run to weeds. But looking at her you'd never have known she'd been in the hospital at all. Her skinny arms were still muscly and brown as an old man, and she walked around in her frightening old bare feet like she'd always done when I was a child, growing up and knowing that other kids at school had fathers who went to work and mothers who wore stockings and lipstick and were pretty.

'A great old bird, your aunt,' someone had said to me once. He was a person who had known my parents, Aunt Eila knew him. He told me he'd brought a present for me that turned out to be a doll in a box with a set of clothes pinned to the cardboard behind her. He patted me on the head when he gave it, a hot and shiny man.

'Grow up like old Eila and you'll be all right in this world,' he said.

I held the doll in the box close to me like I loved it but really I'd been hoping he might have given me a photograph instead, of me as a baby and my parents holding me and smiling for the camera and being in love.

'Cat got your tongue?' Eila had her hand on me,

grasping. There would be no photographs. She would be my familiar.

After the long taxi drive to the outskirts of town, it was late afternoon when I arrived back in her house. She was sitting in her favourite chair, at her needlepoint, as if I'd never been away. Her feet were their own creatures, like monkeys. The toes fiddled and danced as she stitched the wool to its thick felt backing, callouses were eyes and noses. This was your aunt, I was thinking. This room, smell. This your family, this person. Those creatures there twitching, yours. The room, hot garden, the day – all of it wanting to be belonging.

'We've had a good summer here, this year,' her voice came strong out of the darkened room, her fingers at the needle. 'You've caught the end of it but still it's deathly hot.'

Outside, the insects were busy. Prick, prick. Under every glossy leaf, they were nestling in thick, busy columns, worked up into the insides of flowers. Their wavering feelers and tiny wet heads would be working busily against the petal's edges.

'What a shame for you. All the boys and girls out in their bathing things and, darling, you look so overheated.'

Prick, prick. She pulled the wool taut, made a knot, bit it clean from the backing with her teeth. All the time, as she worked, her brown feet moved with their own thoughts. Her whole body was alive with thoughts, thoughts glinted off the little pearls she'd always worn. Ideas about me were in her tiny bright eyes.

Years away from her, travelling back through days and nights and seasons . . . None of it could put space between here and then. I was hers again like I'd never left, my poor lipstick all undone.

'I have a good job there, Aunt E. I make lots of money. I live in a nice flat with some nice people, I . . .'

She was threading up, another pig in a stable, another

trapped plant for a cushion or a footstool. Her needlepoint in frames behind glass filled the silent spaces on the walls. Needlepoint at my back, my hard sofa.

'I . . . I . . .'

But why even try to speak? When her little pearls were eyeing me for lies? How to talk about my own life? The things I did to earn my money?

It's a smart place. I got the job walking in off the streets. It's an Italian restaurant, it's in Knightsbridge, and I first noticed it because of the windows which were huge and opaque like they'd been dipped in milk. Outside the entrance was a stand of oriental trees, thin thin branches I'd never seen before. At night they were strung with tiny white fairytale lights that touched and glittered.

I started out as water boy, making sure the glasses were fresh, clearing plates. Some people say it's the hardest part of a restaurant job.

Then, after weeks, my boss moved me up to waiting tables and I kept a tiny map tucked in my belt to remember the seating plan. There were special phrases – 'What can I do for you tonight?' – and different kinds of smiles. The money was good. Soon I could afford to buy expensive shoes, narrow, dark shoes with long heels that I could wear at work because then I was taking my time more, learning how to be a hostess and how to play.

I smiled at all the dark haired men who were our customers. They were uniformly handsome with skin and eyes that were cleaned and buffed, their bodies done up in shirts and suits pressed into lines. Sometimes they brought their girlfriends to the restaurant with them, or their wives, and I smiled at those too, paid them the little compliments. Other nights they were alone, on a Monday, say, or a Wednesday, late and then I would often go home with one of them. They kept hard beds, those men, but their lovemaking had a kind of liquidity that pleased me at the

time. After it, I'd leave early, take the tube back to South
London, and go home for my own sleep. I used to wake late
in the afternoon, with ideas.

This was my life, then. My own chapters and sentences,
no sing-song memories. There was no crying in it. Aunt
Eila wrote me letters that arrived once a month like
bleeding, but I'd trained myself to think less and less about
the contents of my body and I could do it with her too.

I had phrases for her that I used in London, when people
asked. *A sweet old thing*, I said. *Completely batty but always
wonderful to me*. After a while, I realized the sentences were
all I needed. I needn't think about her at all or the place
where I used to live.

I felt safe. Like in a circus, with your own rules, safe like a
box. I felt I was beginning a life, that I could be anybody. I
really did believe I could step out, be so smart. A person
might think, how young to believe that, a person might
think how vain. They would have known, wouldn't they,
that eventually a letter would arrive, claiming me back.

Oh, wasn't she ill now, strung up with the operation. Oh,
didn't she hate the pills, hate the nurses, hate the day. Every
word on the thin airmail paper crawled with intimacy; I was
hers as if I really was a daughter. Why cheat myself that I
had a chance to play with ropes, let myself be swung, when
one day I'd be sitting in her darkness again, silent as a child.

'Should've brought your swimming things. What's the
use of earrings or that fancy bag of clothes now that you're
home? Who's going to see you in fancy pants except me and
I don't need impressing.'

She blindly bit another thread and bent again to the
work.

'Remember me,' she said. 'I already know all about your
skinny little body . . .'

A prick into tearing, that's how it starts. Remembering
again. It's all happening again. Stepping off the plane, the

air sucking up to meet you, can anyone avoid a homecoming? And things you see, a car window glinting in the sunlight, the fall of a piece of sky, remind you. Then you're plucking out an old woman's eyebrows, tweezing her chin . . . You're doing what you're told. Or you're standing up on a chair to fasten her bra before you yourself have got dressed for school . . . But you don't think it's so queer. None of these memories have to hold, you don't have to keep them banging in your head. Perhaps they never happened, you never did it, it's not real. Even the punishments she invented that were different every time, they could be just another sentence on the page.

And now, look at me. Now I'm the hostess. I'm the one who greets. When people come into the restaurant I take their coats and show them to their tables like it's my own party they've been invited to. And I wear the most beautiful things. Fitted black dresses in cashmere and silk underwear beneath. At home, the flat I share is clean and light and painted in pale colours. The TV, video, telephone . . . all of it is modern. I spend hours talking to my friends about books and films and restaurants they've been to. I think about having my own boyfriend instead of letting my body get more messy with sex. Or maybe just stopping it. Maybe moving out and buying my own place.

These things are my life, the thick pale carpets, scent, new shoes . . . So why did an old woman's gizzardy neck and threads mean anything? What was my dressed body doing there, in a squint wooden house half strangled by tropical vines? Outside the shaded window, the hills and mountains were pressing in – but why claim me? What did my little outfits have to do with a country of mutton bones scattered through gardens? Of meat and fish heads wrapped in newspaper and buried in shallow graves?

On the plane, the stewardesses' faces had split with smiles through their suntans.

'How nice that you're coming home . . .'

Touching down, over the bony back of the North Island, the forced air of the cabin pressed against the bright blue miles outside the window. Gorsey hump-backed hills swung over my left shoulder, the white mountain in the distance tipped into the churning sea.

I couldn't have told you why I'd come. If you'd asked, I couldn't have told.

'Is everything all right?' asked the stewardess. 'Can I get you something for pain?'

'Whew . . .' The overweight man at passport control whistled when he saw the date on my visa. 'Long time, no see, little girl. You're all grown up too, won't your father whistle . . .'

I grappled with my hand luggage, not looking for anything, just because the leather was so beautiful. New looking and clean, even though it had travelled all that way.

'I'm only here for two weeks . . .' said my voice. 'It's only a holiday. It's only –'

'Hey, easy. I'm only asking, you know? Just relax . . .' He continued to finger my passport, licking, turning the pages over and over. When he came to the photograph, he looked at me, full on.

'All grown up, eh? . . . '

My own face replied, *Please let me go*.

Kill them all. It's not as if I was there for a history, or for photos, or to find a set of memories I could keep. I didn't want a bit of their earth, some colour of sky. I didn't need an aunt, dark house, the stink of unmentionable meats. I'd made myself forget about all that long since. Made myself, like being sick. I'd already got rid of it, being her special kept and secret little girl, I was nearly clean of it. Nor was there anything left in the house to remember me by. If you visited there today, you would never know I had lived there. There would be no clues.

Even the photograph albums had empty pages. There were darker squares where the pictures had been and on some pages fragments of sellotape lay like fingernails. And things I'd played with – dolls – there was nothing in my old room.

Since I'd gone she'd turned it into a kind of guest house, with a blanket on the thin bed that she'd knitted herself from old scraps – not my own eiderdown, or any of my soft pillows. In the wardrobe there were just empty wire coat hangers, a little ruined choir. There were no clothes and the box at the top that had held the dressing-up things and my mother's wedding dress was stuffed full only of yellowing tissue paper.

Eila said she'd burnt everything because she couldn't stand it, that when I'd left she'd wanted me out, and that's how she'd done it. Made a fire and thrown everything in.

'You little bitch . . .'

I didn't mind what she said, I'd forgotten it.

'Little animal . . .'

I didn't mind, didn't. The sound of a million screaming insects came from the vegetables and thick flowers and matted bushes where they lived. I didn't mind at all what she'd said. It would be an easy thing to change my ticket, be back in London the day after tomorrow like I'd never been away, the visit never happened.

'Who do you think you are? Coming back here and expecting things? Who do you think wants to see you?' She had put down her tapestry now and was looking. Her little pearls squinted at me off her chest. She still held the tiny needle.

'There's nobody wants to see you, and that's the answer.

You've wasted all your money. All your fanciness . . . wasted.'

She picked up her work again, she was exhausted, she was too old for tricks. I rose to make a cup of tea.

'It's been a good year here one way or another,' she said. 'A hot summer, the farmers are happy and so are my shares.' She looked at me then and I knew she'd be wanting to hold me, kiss me. 'I'm not ready to sell up yet. One day, darling. All this will be yours . . .'

The woolly thing in her lap heaved as she spoke. It was late afternoon and summer was ending for her. The green curtains hung like hair; the only light was a slice of yellow, like pollution, on the wall behind her head. Her curdled halo, it was what she deserved. Her end of summer, my spring.

I had always kept myself so quiet in that dark house, but now it was my turn for seed. I'd stayed virgin so long. Staying in that house, in that country, I'd waited out my time. Practising scales at the piano, removing my clothes for bed at night, cleaning plates after lunch. I was seventeen once, and all the girls from school were wearing brown foundation on their faces and mascara. They perched on the high spindly stools at the café bar in Rublyeff's Department Store. Boys were there too, with tongues, but not for me. I kept myself so quiet in my own dark room.

Yet I was pretty, wasn't I? I could have been a star? I could have played in concert halls all over the world. Met my friends for lunch and gone shopping for clothes that came packaged in cardboard boxes and shiny paper bags. I could have been a daughter, found friends. Had a man to fall in love with and a wedding made of net curtains and pale gorse torn from the hills.

If I'd wanted it, I could have parted the curtains and let

sunlight into the dark house, just for pleasure. I could have had the garden, its fevered flowers and bush, and the land beyond the clay gorge where the sheep tangled in branches and were caught, bleating, drowning in slimy mud when it rained.

I made Aunt Eila her cup of tea, cream and honey as she liked it. I stayed on with her for the two weeks, saw no one. I sat with her most days, indoors. The curtains were drawn and hushed while the weather outside was persistent, great loud crying blue days that never let up. My aunt didn't say anything I would remember. She'd be dead soon anyhow.

I made one visit out. But the café bar at Rublyeff's had been turned into a shoe department selling boots with spiky heels and racks of socks and tights in ugly colours.

There were no more spindly chairs where the girls had sat, twinkling under the chandeliers, filling their mouths with cream. There were no chairs where I had sat with Aunt Eila when she took me there for a treat when I was still too young to know better, to know that I was marking time in my dark bedroom, sleeping, keeping myself safe for leaving.

I don't know why I've chosen these things to talk about. I don't know why you should be interested. For godsake, you're a stranger too. Where is your home? Where were you born?

I am a waitress in a bar.
I am the one who greets, the one who smiles at the customers as she takes their dark coats.
I wear expensive accessories, underthings.
I live in London.
I am that woman.

The Lemon Tree

BROOKE AUCHINCLOSS-FOREMAN

Did I know her they asked me. Blue lights were flashing in my eyes. It was cold and I could see my breath and the red lights of the ambulance and the white sheets over her. They were trying to find her family, did I know anything – it really would help.

Her dream was the same each time. The sun was shining and she was there, as a little girl. Her mother and her sisters were there. They were wearing black and their faces were heavily made-up. They were dancing in a circle, holding hands and singing and laughing. Then a bell began to toll loudly, and suddenly the sky grew pitch black and giant yellow flower petals fell from the sky. The air was thick with them. She was laughing and happy but the heavy yellow petals stuck to her skin blistering and burning her. She ran away from the house and as she ran she saw a road sign – it was in English but she couldn't make out the meaning of the words. She woke up sweating.

It was cold in her room and her white nightgown stuck to her cold skin. She tore it off and changed quickly in the darkness; she put on a thin, woollen sweater and lit a cigarette. For an hour or more she sat in the dark, watching the smoke from her cigarettes drift slowly towards the cracked ceiling of her one-room apartment.

Elaine drove a petrol blue Plymouth Dart. The right

front wing had been smashed in and it rubbed against the wheel as she drove. The skylight too had been smashed in and she'd taped a large, used envelope over the hole. It was November and a cold wind whistled through the gaps in the roof.

She stopped at a red light and rummaged in the plastic compartment under her car radio. A tape with no label, an old Chapstick, some pennies, a broken hairbrush, two empty 'Lifesaver' wrappers, a blue leather glove . . . the search failed to find what she was after and Elaine dumped the contents of her handbag onto the passenger seat. A nylon scarf, another broken hairbrush, two cassette tapes, a datebook stuffed with bits of paper, some odd keys, a tampon, a broken eye-liner pencil and a dilapidated looking lipstick. The car swerved slightly as she applied pink lipstick to her broad lips. She looked in the rearview mirror and brushed back her long black hair. There were dark circles under her eyes and her olive skin was blotchy and uneven.

She parked the car under a streetlight in a rough, industrial part of the city and slipped on a pair of golden sandals. It was seven-thirty and her class should have started fifteen minutes ago.

Inside the students eyed her warily as they took off their brightly-coloured jumpers and fleece-lined thermal jackets. She apologized and fumbled in her bag for a tape. The class consisted of seven rather dowdy older women from the other side of town. None of them were past forty but all of them had melted into soft round shapes which they sought to hide under baggy t-shirts and *casual* silk shirt-dresses. She had danced at a demonstration at the local Mall and one by one they had ventured forth, sheepishly, to sign up for her class.

Before the class they giggled to each other, tugging nervously on pink stockings stretched too tightly over large thighs. '– My husband would just die if he knew I was here,' said one lady while she imagined herself as a slim, Middle Eastern Mata Hari, gyrating around her bedroom to the amazement of her husband. She tried not to look in the mirrored wall in front of her.

Elaine stuffed a cassette into the stereo the wrong way round and it ground to a halt, clicking loudly through the scratchy PA system. The students covered their ears. She flipped the tape and as the music began Elaine felt a warm, familiar power surging through her. Slowly and dramatically but without deliberation she wrapped a long, red nylon scarf around her hips, and arranged its long tassles to run along her slim thigh. 'This music,' she explained without looking up, 'is Arabic. The song is the song of the lover who loses his love.' Her voice had a hypnotic lull to it and the ladies stopped fidgeting and watched her intently as she slipped her sandals off and walked gracefully to the front of the room, carefully placing one foot in front of the other as she walked.

She stood with her back to the class facing the mirrored wall. Some of the ladies in the class stood a little straighter as they looked at Elaine's square shoulders in front of them. The voice on the tape began to softly wail and Elaine's hips began to move gently – the class following her instinctively. They swayed as she swayed and followed every move of her body carefully, jealously, admiringly, with their eyes – their faces were taut and eager.

'– Here the lover calls to his love – "*you have left me and I am like a bird with a broken wing . . . the sun does not shine for me . . .*"' As she spoke the words of the song, the music began to carry Elaine like a leaf in the wind – away from the class, and away from the city. The muscles in her stomach quivered, echoing the sobbing voice of the man on the tape, she was drifting away slowly '". . . *there is no moon*",' she whispered. Her back arched and her arms swung softly by

her sides. The women behind her moved awkwardly and
self-consciously, like lazy, overweight clowns imitating a
graceful animal but they were watching Elaine as if she held
the secret to eternal life.

'*". . . I stand at the end of the earth . . ."*' She didn't think
about them – tonight the music seemed to sink deep inside
her, spilling over, flooding her, taking her over. Her body
heaved and sunk, and the cymbals on her fingers chimed
unconsciously to the music.

She was the little girl in her dream again and it was her
thirteenth birthday. She rose quickly from the floor and
skipped lightly away from the mirrored wall at the front of
the room – the class followed – faithful and unaware. When
Elaine spoke now, she heard her mother's voice – 'This
song is the coming of age song and today you are a woman
. . . the dance teaches you about controlling your body –
your arms, your breasts, your pelvic muscles . . .' Elaine's
class smiled shyly.

Looking in the mirror Elaine could see her mother in a
long black dress standing before her. She could hear her
mother's voice in Arabic now – low and soft. When she
looked down, Elaine saw her bare feet on the hard, soft dirt
floor of her mother's house and she stamped them proudly,
the way she had done on her thirteenth birthday. The
music played cheerily on.

She tossed her head and shook the scarf at her hips. She
was with her mother and her sisters again now, dancing in a
circle. The tape continued but Elaine was frozen in another
place, she moved effortlessly to the music but storm clouds
were gathering in her mind as the class blindly imitated her
every move.

A heavy drum pounded loudly in her head. Now it was
nighttime and she was seventeen. She saw her father's face
and she saw the faces of other men flickering in the firelight.
They held her and she struggled. As the drum beat, Elaine

began to arch slowly backward till her long hair touched the floor. She looked up at the leaves of the lemon tree against the dark sky and she shut her eyes tight.

Elaine swung her torso around and around and the ladies of the class did the same. Now she was in a hurricane, whirling, madly spinning in its centre – powerless. She circled the room, striking the floor with the end of her long scarf. The song ended and Elaine stopped dead in her tracks, head down, arms at her sides, she was breathing hard and dripping with sweat.

The tape was over and the class was over. The students applauded and began to gather their things.

'No,' I answered, 'I didn't know her.'

Southern Comfort

AUDREY THOMAS

Elizabeth has flown across a continent because her mother decided to starve herself to death. Now she sits in the nondescript waiting room of the bus depot at White River Junction waiting for her sister to pick her up. It's mid February and there's lots of fresh snow outside the glass windows. Elizabeth loved snow as a child and some of her happiest memories are of winter: sledding at night, making snowmen (always called 'snowmen', she thinks now, even when snow women, snow children or snow dogs) or making forts. Seeing the snow outside, seeing men stamping their feet and breath coming like smoke from people's mouths she has a stab of pure nostalgia. But snow is really for children and skiers, not for people who have to shovel out the driveway and then maneuver cars on icy roads; she wouldn't move back east for the world.

There's a big yellow bow on both doors of the bus depot and the headlines in newspapers in the vending machines outside are full of news of the War. Elizabeth's sister Nancy is on her second marriage – to a much younger man. Nancy always makes a big point of this – that she has 'caught' a much younger (good-looking, sexy) guy and now that he's been called up she's very proud. At this very moment, Elizabeth thinks, looking at the clock above the change machine, he must be getting ready to chow down out there in California, at Desert Palm or whatever ridiculous name they've given the embarcation center. Mike isn't that

young; in fact he's not really young at all – he's forty-six,
old enough to have been in Vietnam only he wasn't, he was
a theological student at the time. Elizabeth is not sure
whether he had to join the Active Marine Reserve because
of this or whether some sort of guilt was involved (all those
contemporaries of his who came home in zipped up bags,
like laundry being sent home to Mommy) but he has been a
faithful weekend soldier once a month for years. He went to
Norway a few years back, for war games. He said one guy
had the job of picking up poop in plastic bags so the 'enemy'
wouldn't know where they'd been. Could that be true?
When Elizabeth visits Nancy and Mike she tends to drink
too much so perhaps she's remembered it wrong – surely
they had portable latrines?

Elizabeth tried to talk to Mike once, about the cruise
missile flights over Canada. 'You Canadians,' he said
smiling (he smiled a lot, Elizabeth's private nickname for
him was 'Mr Sociable') 'you Canadians just want to sit up
there and let us keep you safe.'

'Who asked you to?' she said. Nancy intervened and said
they weren't to talk politics, it upset her.

This exchange took place during the Reagan era. Mike
thought the world of Reagan because he had been so
wonderful when the dead marines had been shipped home
from Lebanon. Nancy, who proclaimed herself a Demo-
crat, said she couldn't agree with Reagan's politics but she
liked the way he treated his wife.

'The way Charlie MacCarthy treated Edgar Bergen?'
Elizabeth said quietly.

'What?' said her sister, who was slightly deaf in one
ear.

'Nothing.'

Nancy asked Mike to freshen her drink.

* * *

Every time Elizabeth came back to the States she realized
she had forgotten a lot of the idioms. Nobody said 'freshen
your drink' in Canada – or nobody she knew. Her sister
(and her sister's grown-up children) had another expression which Elizabeth had never heard – perhaps it was
strictly New England: 'I was really bullshit' meaning 'I was
furious.' It seemed self-contradictory but they all used it.
Elizabeth, who had married an English man, and then
emigrated to Canada, felt she was more or less fluent in
three kinds of idiomatic English but this phrase she didn't
know. Her own children, when small, moved easily
between biscuit and cookie, sweetie and candy, wellies and
gum boots, serviettes and napkins. Elizabeth herself knew
the very real differences between 'certified' in England and
'certified' in North America, between 'caravan' and 'caravan', 'homely' and 'homely'. These were the ones that
could get you into trouble. Canadian English seemed to be
a combination of the two plus several idioms of its own:
'make strange' ('Does your baby make strange,' said an old
woman to Elizabeth her first week in British Columbia),
'messages', 'bring up'. Elizabeth was a literary journalist
with her own show on the CBC: she was very interested in
words and how they were used. She spent her working life
interviewing writers and critics. 'I'm an instant expert on
aboriginal short stories,' she told her friends or 'ask me
about the woman who was the Margaret Lawrence of
Japan.' It bothered her that she never had much time to
study anything in depth and she thought from time to time
of quitting and doing something less superficial. But she
liked meeting people, the pay was all right (by Canadian
standards) and she got to travel a lot. Now that her children
and husband had all 'flown the coop' as she liked to put it,
she was free to travel whenever the opportunity arose. In
fact, she is due in Australia in exactly ten days. Two days
ago she explained to the organizers of her visit, that

whether she arrived or not depended a great deal on what happened with her mother. The telephone connection was very bad. The person at the other end thought she said 'brother'. 'I hope your brother is better soon.' 'Mother,' she shouted, 'mother,' but the line had gone dead. They probably thought she had a brother dying of AIDS.

After last year's visit, as her sister and Mike were driving her to the station, Nancy said, 'So, are you seeing anyone?'

'Not really,' Elizabeth said and wished she didn't feel ashamed at not being able to trot out some bright new lover.

'But you meet all these interesting *people*,' Nancy said, meaning interesting *men*.

'I don't really meet them; I interview them for half an hour. Sometimes I interview them over the phone, never even see their faces, except on the jackets of their books – and you can't trust that.'

'No men hey,' said her sister. 'What are you, a "Les"?'

Elizabeth couldn't believe what she'd just heard. If she wasn't with a man, she was probably a lesbian – and therefore, from the tone of voice – inferior, kinky. A few minutes ago Mike had been talking about a bank manager who'd given him some trouble, a woman. 'Mike says she's an ex-nun,' Nancy told her, from the front seat. 'He can always spot them – because he went to theological college.'

(He's going to say underfucked and over forty, Elizabeth thought.)

'Underfucked and over forty,' Mike said to the windscreen/windshield.

(Did Les's *fuck*? Could she reply that if the woman was a Les she might not be underfucked? To the best of her knowledge, no one had come up with a good etymological explanation of 'fuck'.)

* * *

Elizabeth was about to get some change for a newspaper when Nancy came hurrying in, 'Come quick, I'm double parked.' As she struggled with her heavy case, packed for beaches as well as blizzards in case she ended up going directly from Montreal to Vancouver to Sydney she watched her sister steam ahead without a backward glance. For years now, ever since a therapist had told her she should be more assertive, Nancy had assumed an aggressive walk. It didn't matter who she was walking with, child, cripple, old person, you had to match your step to hers or be left behind. There was something in the way she put her feet down, almost a stamp. It was not, in fact, an attractive walk but it certainly was effective – Nancy covered great distances in very little time. If you were left behind, on the other side of the red light, or wondering which of three corners she'd disappeared around, that was your problem, not hers. As Elizabeth had never seen her sister as anything *but* assertive, she wondered about the therapist who had given her this advice.

No. That wasn't true. It began when they were tee-nagers, after Nancy and Elizabeth had not been pledged to their mother's old sorority.

Elizabeth retreated into moody shyness but Nancy joined the drama club and took on a new persona – lots of lipstick, tight sweaters, lots of boys from the second-best families. She was a good actress – she always played 'character' parts, wisecracking maids or Irish maids or old ladies – perhaps she was acting now. Perhaps what she had told that therapist was that she was afraid, that her life was out of control. Perhaps the walk was like a built-up shoe – it kept her steady and no one would notice the limp.

As Elizabeth heaved her case into the back of the station wagon her sister said: 'She's eating now – or drinking at least. I tried to get you last night but you'd already left.'

'I spent the night in Montreal; I'd given you the number, remember?'

'Oh, I forgot. Anyway, I'm glad you're here. It's been crazy with Mike leaving and mother pulling this – I'm a basket case, I really am.'

Elizabeth thought of some of the 'props' (thinking about Nancy's high school acting made the word 'props' come to mind) she had brought with her – a Bible, some sprigs of rosemary, a yellow candle, a new white pillowcase with a crocheted edge; if her mother had chosen to 'go out' Elizabeth thought it would be fitting to have some small ceremony to the event itself – the going out – since there wasn't to be a funeral. Cremation, their mother had said. Would Nancy divide the ashes equally or would they have some sort of time-share system, six months in Vermont, six months in British Columbia? Stop it, Elizabeth told herself, that's not funny.

Nancy pointed out the veterans' hospital as they drove through town to the convalescent hospital.

'They're expanding,' she said. 'A lot of the boys may not come back the same as when they left.' Nancy said this cheerfully or perhaps dramatically. Elizabeth glanced at her sister's face but she was concentrating on her driving.

'I thought this was going to be a short, sharp war or something like that?'

'Who knows? They told Mike to go home and make his will.' She pulled sharply into the parking lot and got out of the car quickly, striding towards the door. Elizabeth was having trouble with her seat belt so Nancy was already inside and down the corridor. It was probably tiredness – the rushing to get packed, the plane trip, the bus ride, but Elizabeth kept having the desire to laugh. As she hurried after her sister (a notice by the door said PLEASE REMOVE BOOTS BEFORE PROCEEDING but as Nancy had ignored this Elizabeth simply pawed at the rubber matting two or three times and kept going) she thought of Alice and the White

Rabbit and a movie she had seen long ago where somebody
says – David Niven – to an ostrich driver – 'Follow that
ostrich!'

An old man in a baseball cap rushed up to her and grabbed
her arm – 'Mickey Mantle,' he shouted in her ear – 'Mickey
Mantle.'

'Mr Oliver,' called a nurse, 'be a good boy and go back to
the sun room. Don't bother the visitors, OK?'

She smiled at Elizabeth as she passed with a towel-
covered tray. You couldn't tell what was underneath – a
snack or a hypodermic syringe or something even worse.

There were wooden handrails along the corridors – to help
the ambulatory patients – to give them something to hold
onto. About every three feet someone had tied a big yellow
bow. This yellow ribbon thing was new – had it started with
the Vietnam war? She knew the song of course but since
when had it been used as a contemporary symbol of
support? There were yellow ribbons after the siege at the
American Embassy in Lebanon – one of the few times
Americans actually said thank you to Canadians – but who
thought it up originally – the revival of yellow ribbons on
doors, yellow ribbons on the aerials of cars, wreaths of
yellow ribbons and American flags in the window of a
florist shop in Burlington. Quite a different thing from
calling someone 'yellow' – 'whyn't you fight like a man you
yellow-bellied coward!' And of course the yellow peril.

The town they grew up in had been ninety-nine percent
white, although their mother would have argued that the
Jews weren't white and the Jews themselves might have

objected to being lumped in with the Gentiles. There was
only one black girl in the high school and she was beautiful
so she was safe. Elizabeth and her family lived on the west
side of town; there were Ukrainians and Polacks but they
stayed on the east side, except for basketball games. Elizabeth couldn't remember ever seeing an East Indian or
anyone Chinese or Japanese. There were probably towns
like this still, but with television in (nearly) every home
children had some sense of a wider world – or did they?
What did the child-on-the-street think of when he or she
heard talk about Iraqis? Did Bush deliberately pronounce
Hussein's name so it came out as 'Sodom?'

Did other cultures refer to their fighting men as 'our
boys?'

Her mother was sitting up in a wheelchair, weeping – or
rather mewing, for that's what it sounded like – little mews
of despair. She didn't have the strength to cry. 'Look who's
here!' Nancy called out in her 'hearty' voice. (Nancy had
learned about projection in her acting days and she still
talked as though she had to reach the people in the back
row.) 'Here's Betsy.'

Her mother looked up, grey-faced, crumpled, her eyes
leaking tears.

'Hello, Mother,' Elizabeth said, and bent to kiss her. Her
mother did not like to be kissed so Elizabeth merely pressed
her lips against the soft, wrinkled cheek. ('Don't kiss me,
dear,' she would say, 'you might get my germs.' Their
mother suffered from continuous colds.)

Tears dripped down her mother's face. 'Tell your sister,'
she said in her tiny voice, 'Tell your sister I can't go on.'
Again that terrible mewing – a kitten in a sack.

'Mother's upset because they've lost her dressing gown,'
Nancy said, 'it didn't come back from the laundry.'

Mother scrabbled at the flowered duster she was wearing.

'This doesn't belong to me – I would never buy such a thing as this. They stole my dressing gown and left me this old thing.'

'Now Mother,' said Nancy. 'It will turn up.'

'After I'm dead,' said Mother.

In early February their mother had fallen in her room and broken her hip. (Or broken her hip and fallen said the doctors: at that age you can't really tell.) She'd come through a hip replacement and was even up for a few shaky minutes every day, a nurse on each side, while they changed her bed. Nancy reported that the doctors said she had the stamina of a woman half her age. Elizabeth had laughed into the telephone receiver: 'Haven't I always said it's the nasty ones who live the longest? All that acid in the system – clears them out like Draino.'

But then she had been transferred from the big hospital in Dartmouth to this small convalescent home. Not so much fussing over her and not so many sedatives to keep away the pain and the fear that she'd be in this place for the rest of her days. A week ago she had gone on her hunger strike and three days ago Nancy had phoned. 'I think she's going.'

Elizabeth noticed, on the night table, a half full glass of something pink. Nancy smiled.

'That's her "milkshake".' She raised her voice, 'You drank half your milkshake didn't you, Ma?'

The old woman looked at Elizabeth in despair. 'She wants me to get better; she won't let me go. Tell her . . . tell her . . .'

Mother shared a room with an old lady who was completely out of it. The curtain was drawn between the two beds

but Elizabeth could see a long bony foot sticking out – a foot
the colour of skim milk but with yellow toe nails – and they
couldn't curtain off the moans and curses.

Would I want to hang on, Elizabeth thought, if I had to
stay in here?

('She probably won't be able to do it,' Elizabeth's doctor
said when she phoned him, 'unless she slips into a coma.
She'll get very thirsty and once she wants to drink they can
put nutrients in her liquids and keep her alive. She's
probably just depressed.'

'I think her doctors have told her they won't stop her if
this is what she wants to do.'

'And I think they've told her that primarily because they
know she won't be able to.')

Now, looking at her mother, she wished there were some
pleasant, unfrightening way she could just drift off to sleep.
(On a soft white pillowcase, with herbs and a yellow candle,
music playing even. Elizabeth had brought a tape recorder
and a tape of 'The Maldou' – just why that recording she
wasn't sure. Because of the sound of the river, perhaps. A
river flowed through the town where they grew up, where
her mother grew up.)

'I can't help you Ma,' Nancy was saying. 'I can help you
to get better, but not the other thing.'

'I've got a tube sticking into me,' her mother said, 'it's so
uncomfortable, oh dear, oh dear.'

Nancy went and got the nurse and they helped her
mother back to bed. Propped up on pillows, with the hated
flowered duster banished, their mother was persuaded to
drink part of a fresh milkshake, and then they left.

'I've *told* her she's in the wing for convalescents, not
extended care,' Nancy said on the way home. 'They
wouldn't have put her there if they didn't think she'd get

better. She looks a hundred times better than she did on Sunday. Mike was crying when he left her; he was convinced we wouldn't see her again.'

'Do you think she really wants to live?'

'She hasn't come to terms with death. Let's just say she doesn't really want to die.'

'Do you?'

'I'm not *afraid*, not like she is.'

'Do you think she's afraid of the Hereafter?'

Nancy nodded. 'Exactly. She's afraid she's going to be judged.'

Nancy was a churchgoer; Elizabeth was not, yet Elizabeth realized that she, too, might have that fear if she were in her mother's place. She too might be afraid she would be judged. A day of reckoning. (Even a half-hour of reckoning might be too awful to contemplate.)

Each day they went to the convalescent home and each day they stopped in the village, on some pretext or other – a loaf of bread at the bakery, a deposit at the bank, a reservation at the Inn – so that Nancy could talk about Mike out there at Desert Palm, learning all about the new weapons before he went overseas. Everyone said, 'Well, we're sure proud of him' or 'Our prayers go with him' and Nancy glowed – there was no other word for it, she glowed. Yellow rosettes in front of the teller's grilles; yellow ribbons on mailboxes. The manufacturers of yellow ribbons must be making a fortune, Elizabeth thought (but not out loud). Each night they watched the television. Elizabeth found it hard to keep her mouth shut. She wanted to say to Nancy, 'What is this war all about; explain it to me, in your own words. What are the Americans *doing* over there?' But the Canadians were going as well – not to fight but to protect and to pick up the wounded so she kept silent, bit her tongue. The grocery bags proclaimed support for our troops.

On Sunday, along with the prayers for the sick (Mother was included) there were prayers for our boys in the Gulf and most particularly for Mike Bryant – we want him home soon and safe and sound. In the vestibule later, along with the cookies and squares and coffee there was talk of babies being murdered, electricity cut off from incubators.

'What about Vietnam,' Elizabeth said, 'what about napalm?' Up to that point everyone had been very welcoming.

'I'm sorry,' Elizabeth said in the car, 'it just slipped out.' The snow was falling thick and fast so Nancy was concentrating on the driving. The explosion came after they were home. Nancy poured herself a generous shot of Jack Daniels and then confronted her sister.

'It really *bothers* me, Betsy, how smug you are, how unpatriotic. Sometimes I'd like to kick you right out of the house.'

'I'm not here to be patriotic,' Elizabeth said. 'I'm here because you said Mother was dying.'

'You don't know *anything*,' Nancy said, and went upstairs to her room and slammed the door.

Elizabeth made herself a sandwich, then bundled up and took the dog for a walk. The dog was another bone of contention. Nancy talked for the dog, and in baby-talk, as though the dog was a lisping five-year-old child, and this Elizabeth absolutely refused to do.

('Auntie Bitsy, Auntie Bitsy, will oo take me for a wittle walk? I need to do pee pee Auntie Bitsy.')

When they came back an hour later Nancy was in the family room, sipping another Jack Daniels and reading *Better*

Homes and Gardens. She was still wearing her Sunday best.

'I'm going out to some friends for supper,' she said to the pages open in front of her. 'I don't like to drive in this weather so the husband is coming to pick me up. There's some stew you can heat up, but don't touch the chops, they're for tomorrow and there's not much skim milk left so don't use any.'

Elizabeth assumed she had been invited as well and was now being punished but she really didn't care. An evening by herself sounded very attractive. She'd watch television or read, make some phone calls on her calling card. She loved hearing the operator say 'Thank you for using A.T. & T.'

'Fine,' Elizabeth said.

'I may be quite late. If you go to bed, be sure to damp down the fire.'

'I will,' Elizabeth said, obedient as any model sister.

'I'm still very angry with you,' Nancy said as she got into her coat and boots ('I told him just to honk three times, not to bother coming in').

'I can understand that,' Elizabeth said, and thought she sounded like a psychiatrist.

'With Mike about to be shipped out!' Nancy said.

'I don't want Mike to get killed or even wounded,' Elizabeth said. 'Believe me, I don't.' She had said a few words to Mike last night, when he phoned. He had sounded more excited than scared, but then, he'd been playing war games for years, waiting for the Real Thing.

'Some things are worth fighting for,' Nancy said, as she picked up her woolen scarf.

Elizabeth didn't reply. She turned off the television set after watching a Vermont father, whose son had been riding in a transport vehicle which blew up, talk about how proud he was of his boy, that he'd had a chance to go over and 'kick ass' for his country. She called the hospital to see

how her mother was ('resting comfortably'; 'give her my
love') then called each of her daughters in turn, just to make
sure they were safe.

Before she went to bed she let the dog out again briefly
and while it ran in delighted circles in the drifts she stood at
the doorway inhaling the cold and watching the big flakes
fall and disappear into the general whiteness piled as far as
she could see. She vowed to try harder to love her sister and
to understand her and not to be so judgemental towards her
native land. 'I treat the United States,' she thought to
herself, 'the way men treat their first wives.' This thought
made her laugh. She called in the dog and went to bed.

After a week her mother had rallied enough so that Elizabeth felt she could safely leave. She gave Nancy, who had
more or less forgiven her for her bad attitude, a long list of
phone numbers where she could be reached in Australia.

Her mother was sitting in a wheelchair in the corridor
when Elizabeth went to say good-bye. For the first time her
mother noticed all the yellow ribbons on the handrails.

'What are all these ribbons for?' she said.

'They're for our boys and girls in the Gulf, Mother,
they're for Mike and all the other brave soldiers.'

Their mother looked at the ribbons and looked at her
daughters standing above her in their outdoors clothes.
'Aren't I a brave soldier?' she said.

Elizabeth didn't know whether to laugh or cry. She bent
down and whispered in her mother's ear, 'The bravest,
braver than the whole lot of them.' Then gave her mother a
kiss, a real smackeroo, which surprised them both.

On the way to the bus depot Nancy wondered if she
should stop and get a yellow ribbon for the dog.

La Vie en Rose

LEENA DHINGRA

As the Citroën glided into Gare des Invalides, where I'd come to leave my father to catch his plane to India, the reality started to dawn on me.

'Papa. If you take this job in India, does it mean we'll actually leave Paris?'

'Oh yes!' My father sounded quite cheerful, glancing at the taxi meter and counting out money from his pocket at the same time. He quickly paid, thanked and was out before the Citroën's suspension could heave its final sigh.

'*Merci Monsieur. Et bon voyage. Monsieur, Mademoiselle.*' The driver was clearly pleased at the size of his gratuity.

My father had flapped through the swivel doors before I'd reached the pavement. He believed in arriving early and travelling light. Better to be half an hour early than one minute late, he'd say. Part of his English colonial upbringing. My mother always maintained that after they were married, she had been unable to understand him until she read George Mikes' *How To Be an Alien* which explained English eccentricities.

I had to run to catch up with him in the lobby.

'Will we go forever?'

'What?'

'I said will we leave Paris forever?' I raised my voice against the noisy backdrop of announcements and echoes.

'Forever eh? What's forever? And what about happily ever after?'

'Stop it Papa. You know what I mean.'

'Well. If we go back to India, we'll go home. Wouldn't you like that?'

I nodded, unsure. 'Home' was an exciting and bewildering idea.

'Don't worry darling! Whatever happens, it will take time. Paris won't be wound up that quickly. You've still got to finish your studies in London. Who knows, it might make more sense to make London the base for a while.'

'And Paris?' I insisted.

'Do you love Paris so much?'

'I never thought about it.' I never needed to, I thought, as I looked around the Invalides and my father checked in. This is where I had arrived, fifteen years earlier aged four. I couldn't remember anything except that I was carrying a huge tin of ghee and my smile was so wide that it hurt, but I couldn't contain it, I was so happy.

'I've left a list of the instructions on Mummy's red Chinese bureau, of things that need to be done in the flat before you leave for London. Cross each out as you complete the task. When you've turned off the gas, cross it off. Are you listening?'

'Don't worry, Papa, I'm not a child! Isn't this where I arrived when I first came?'

'What?' We were walking towards the coaches.

'When I first came to Paris, that very first time, isn't this where I arrived, here, at Les Invalides?'

'Oh then! No. No. We went to the airport to fetch you.'

'Oh.' But the Invalides I decided was still familiar.

'Both Jacques and Marie Thérèse will call. Ask them for anything you might need.'

'Yes Papa.'

'Ok then, bye bye darling. I'm sure you'll enjoy yourself

on your own.' He smiled. 'Oh yes! Whistle to your heart's content wherever you like, but preferably not within Madame Nicole's hearing. She's old and set in her ways and you know how important it is to keep the concierge happy. It's part of living in Paris.'

I strolled around in the Invalides for quite some time after my father's departure. There was always something comforting, familiar about airports and air-terminals. They gave me a sense of purpose and security. I was there with a definite destination – usually home, somewhere. In London, I came 'home' at the end of the day. During the holidays, I came 'home' to Paris and family. And once every two years, we went 'home' to India on 'Home Leave'. India was 'real home', and yet, paradoxically, it was the one place we didn't have a home of our own any more. We always stayed as guests. Of course we'd had a home once, but, when India was divided, it was all lost – the house, the city, everything. I couldn't remember anything.

It was a spring afternoon. The trees were in bloom. And I would take a bus home. Buses were more expensive than the Metro, but my father had left me two whole carnets of bus tickets, plenty for my remaining week in the city. One week, in Paris, all on my own. I smiled at the thought. It was strange the way this holiday had developed. I'd come to spend the three weeks of Easter with my parents when my mother was called away to Switzerland to nurse a sick relative, and now suddenly, my father had to go off to India! It was all decidedly odd, like the disappearance of the Duchess. I climbed into the bus and sat down. Of course Paris was still there, but then again, for how long? The bus jolted. I settled on my seat. There was a lot I needed to think about. After all, Paris is the city of my childhood!

Memories of anything before are too faint. It is here that
memory begins . . .

'*Tickets s'il-vous-plaît mademoiselle!*'

'*Oh, pardon monsieur. Voilà.*'

Where does memory begin? Blowing soap bubbles next
to a railing in a pink frock and white socks. I left my seat
inside the bus and moved to the open platform at the back. I
leaned against the railing, stuck my head out into the
Parisian air to let the Paris wind blow around and through
my head and hair. I closed my eyes and took a deep breath –
mostly of the Gauloises of my fellow travellers.

'*Attention.* You're leaning too far out.'

I opened my eyes and smiled back at the conductor. The
bus was driving along the Tuileries gardens. 'Li Jahdey di
twillrie' as my mother mispronounced it.

On Thursday afternoons she would take me to the
'Jahdeys' for the *Guignol* puppet show. I would skip in zig
zags around her, singing:

> *Maman les petits bateaux*[1]
> *Qui vont sur l'eau*
> *Ont-ils des jambes?*

'Mam lati bato . . .'

'No. No! Not that one! you're supposed to sing the next
one.

> *Mais non mon gros bêta*[2]
> *S'ils en avaient ils marcheraient.*

'Ma noo moo goo bita silanamachara.'

---

[1] Mummy do the boats on the water have legs?

[2] No, little stupid, if they did they'd walk.

My mother's French was nearly as bad as her singing. She sang everything in the same off key monotone. I couldn't remember not speaking French and I tried to teach my mother, to roll her rr's and get her u's, sometimes patiently, sometimes stamping my feet, but to my childish dismay she could never get it right.

There were two gardens: the Jardins des Tuileries and the Jardin du Luxembourg. Both had their *Guignols*. The one in the Luxembourg gardens had a proper theatre which could be closed up and darkened. But it was further away from home, and I was usually taken to the Tuileries. There the *Guignol* was in a large open tent and when the show started the canvas wings would flap down and enclose us. Sitting on the edge of the wooden benches I would scream with all the others: '*Guignol! Guignol! Attention!*' My mother, who would not understand a word of the puppet show, would look dreamily into a distance, her mind far away, in another land, another life. But when the soldier would come to get *Guignol* I would grab her arm and scream with the others, prompting her to do the same. 'Gino, Gino!' she'd cry out.

All those years in Paris, and my mother never learned French and whatever little she knew she mispronounced most terribly. But it never prevented her from getting around and doing whatever she wanted. Dressed in her rich silks and woven Cashmere shawls, she looked stunning, *La belle Indienne*, whom everyone seemed to have the patience to help.

'They say the Parisians are rude. What rude? I've never found a single rude one. Never!'

I decided not to change buses at the Concorde and to get off a few stops earlier in the Rue de Rivoli and then walk the rest of the way home. I got off outside W.H. Smith's – one of my father's rendezvous points where he used to bring me when I was younger. I would go straight to the comics. I was allowed the *Classics Illustrated* and the funnies but not the nasties. But anyway W.H. Smith didn't sell any of the real nasties. I knew what the real nasties were: at home was a thick learned book by a Dr Wertham called *Seduction of the Innocent* and in it were samples of really real nasties.

Occasionally my father would meet someone for one of his regular weekly or monthly columns for Indian papers. Then we'd have tea, and I would acquire a few new comics with which to 'sit quietly' while they talked. He usually referred to these people as 'thinkers'.

'Well he does all sorts of things,' he would explain. 'He's a thinker. He writes, he gives talks, does some teaching.'

The Paris of my childhood was full of 'thinkers' with whom I shook hands and exchanged smiles, and sometimes puzzled over names. And now I smiled at the memory of my confusion about Ionesco and Unesco. My father had laughed.

'No no. He's not named after Unesco. They've got nothing to do with each other. Unesco is the organization. His name is *I*onesco, and it's a Romanian name.'

'Is he a thinker too papa?'

'Oh yes. He writes plays. There's one on now.'

In the city my father spoke in French, English and sometimes German, at home he spoke in English or Punjabi.

Walking down in the sheltered arcades of the Rue de Rivoli thinking: Paris is so pretty!, I saw my *parfumerie*. Marie Thérèse, who translated my father's writings, had brought me there when I was sixteen to buy me my first perfume and lipstick. It had felt like an initiation. They'd fluttered around me, admired my hair, my sari, my skin, my smile. I was instructed as to what was sweet, heavy, languid, green, young, day, soirée. I left with Houbigant's Quelques Fleurs and my first lipstick, Bois de Rose of Lancôme. As I walked on I remembered that year my mother had also been away nursing the same sick relative from India. The tentacles of obligation of the extended Indian family stretched over oceans and continents to lay claim. I stiffened at that idea. But there were nice arcades in New Delhi too, lots of them, all around the Connaught Circus. But I didn't know my way around there. Not like here, in Paris. My Paris!

Past the Concorde, with its silver fountains, and Cleopatra's needle in the whirlpool of traffic, I came into the Avenue des Champs Elysées and as I walked up it I started to feel like the star in my own movie *Hello Paris/Adieu Paris* starring: Maya.

The Champs Elysées was cinemas and strolls, eating *café Liègeois* on the side walk, *The New York Herald Tribune*, shoeshines and Sundays. In the evenings we'd often stroll down it, wander in its arcades, and bring our guests to sit in its cafés as an after-dinner outing. And sometimes, if it got late, we'd pop into the *Herald Tribune* office nearby where the paper came out at 11 p.m. The Champs Elysées was walking distance from our flat.

Across the Arc de Triomphe down the Avenue Mac Mahon, came our *quartier*. It had everything needed in it or very nearby. Two small general stores, a market bursting with fresh fruit and vegetables, cinemas, including one which showed un-dubbed films, restaurants, cafés, shops of every kind, including the Gaylord Hauser health shop and of course Rosine's.

'*Salut* Rosine,' I called out and waved.

Rosine sold records. Her shop, aptly named La Micro-boutique, was no more than a narrow corridor lined high with records on both sides. Two people could just about stand alongside. At the back Rosine, perched on her stool step ladder, waved for me to stop as she came to the door.

'*Salut* Maya. Your father left OK?'

'Yes. He left OK.'

'Freedom eh! Listen, come back in about an hour or so. I can shut for a while and we can take a coffee. OK?'

'OK.'

'You know, we still haven't seen the Duchess.' She winked. 'Speak to you later.'

I turned into the Avenue Niel, past the Magasins Réunis where they made sweets in the entrance; ropes of glistening sugar skilfully pulled, coiled, twisted, turned, changing colour every time until they were chopped mouthsize and left to cool. At the Café Niel I bought myself a strawberry ice cream and though I was almost home I decided to wander through the familiar back streets where I licked, looked at the shops and hoardings: *Laiterie Parisienne, Boulangerie, Pâtisserie, Dubo- Dubon- Dubonnet*, and hummed old nursery rhymes. '*C'est la Mère Michel Qui a perdu son chat!*'

'Mama, where do you buy bread in English?'

'I don't know darling.'

Eleven years old, I was trying to answer test questions for my new boarding school in England.

'What am I supposed to do? It says here to fill in the names of the shops in which I'd buy bread, milk, vegetables, sugar and nails. How can I possibly know what they are if I've never been to England? Mam-ma are you listening?'

My mother lifted her head languidly from scribbling in her notebook. She was always drawing plans of houses to replace the one which had been lost. 'I don't know darling. Ask your father when he comes back from the office.'

'But I've got to finish this now-oo.'

My mother looked up again. 'Well then why don't you write the names in French?'

'You mean write *Boulangerie* and *Laiterie* and things.'

'Yes. And when you get to England you can ask what they are in English.'

Mireille, my hopscotch friend in our previous *quartier*, had thoroughly disapproved of my learning English, but would still play with me because I wasn't English. The English and the Germans, she confided to me, were bad and wicked, *mauvais et vilains*, she said and stamped her foot. The first because they had killed Joan of Arc and the latter because 'they had nicked Aix-la-Chapelle and now claimed it as theirs.'

I didn't understand and Papa said not to try – something about old European rivalries. I wondered where Mireille was now. We used to play in our *tabliers d'école*, our school pinafores, dark blue with deep pockets. And Yves her brother who wanted me to be on his side when we played castles so that he could try and get his hand under my pinafore.

Rosine shut the shop and put a note saying where we were. 'We won't go to Le Vigier, we'll go next door, then I can keep an eye out for customers. Come.'

'What news of the Duchess?'

Rosine shook her head dramatically. From where we were sitting we could see Le Vigier, the imposing *café tabac* on the corner. *Café tabacs* sold cigarettes and stamps, others didn't. 'You see, she's not there. And it is her time.'

Le Vigier looked strangely empty without the familiar figure of La Duchesse. The *garçon* brought our two coffees. Small and black. I didn't particularly like black coffee but thought it was a grown up taste to acquire, so I persevered, trying to keep my grimaces at its bitterness well hidden.

'I tell you she's disappeared. We haven't seen her for more than two weeks! I asked Le Loup, the wolf, he didn't know either.' Rosine waved her arms about her dramatically, *à la parisienne*, shrugging her shoulders and throwing away *zut, flute* and *merde*, left, right and centre. I mirrored. I knew the slangs and intonations. In Paris, I became a *Parisienne* and no one questioned the fact. Rosine was my only friend in the *quartier*. I'd got to know her three years earlier during a long post-'O' level stay and we corresponded while I was away. She kept me informed of the gossip of the *quartier* and in doing so, made me feel a part of it, knowing that others may well be talking about me as we were of them. The Duchess was one of our local colourfuls. Rosine had invented the nickname. There were others: the wolf, the crab, the rose, but La Duchesse was special. She was colourful in every way. Her dyed red hair was piled high on her head and lacquered into a dome, and wisps of curls framed her heavily made-up face. Her lipstick always clashed. She strode down the street gently swinging an umbrella, or a parasol in summer, nodding majestically at the odd greeting. Nobody stared, she was just part of the scene, part of *l'habitude*, the usual.

'She can't just disappear,' protested Rosine, throwing her arms into the air.

Neither of us had ever spoken to the Duchess and we had only recently come to know her real name:

'Madame Verlaine.'

'Verlaine. Do you think she could be related to the poet?'

Rosine nodded thoughtfully. 'Maybe, yes.'

Every afternoon, without fail, *Madame la Duchesse* would walk down the Avenue de Ternes into Le Vigier, and seat herself at a table near the plate glass front from where she could survey the scene. She would stay there some two or three hours, mostly alone, but occasionally joined by someone for a short while. Sometimes she would come twice a day, for breakfast as well. Suddenly, she had not been seen for two weeks. Such a thing had never happened before. Everyone, according to Rosine, remarked on it but no one knew what had happened.

'It is a mystery. Extraordinary! You see Maya I'm so used to seeing her there. She's been there every day since I opened the shop three and a half years ago. And now she's gone! *Pfft partie!*'

'Like an illusion?' I ventured.

Rosine nodded absently as she looked across.

'That's what Maya means: illusion!'

Rosine smiled. 'Maya? Illusion?'

I nodded. 'Do you think anyone would notice if I left the *quartier*?'

'Well. You're always here and then away. But then you always come back regularly.'

I told Rosine the reasons for my father's trip to India.

'*Merde*,' she replied grimacing, shaking her head and shrugging her shoulders at the same time. 'Hell of a long way to go to meet for a coffee.'

We kissed each other the mandatory three times; right, left, right.

'Don't worry *ma vieille*. You might be called Maya, but you are no illusion! *A demain!*'

'*A demain!*'

I bought myself half a *baguette*, some *saucisson* and went home, nibbling on the bread as I walked.

Madame Nicole, our *concierge*, was sitting on the bench outside the apartment block. I slowed my pace. Paris was run by a network of *concierges*. A web across the city. Spiders. And we poor apartment dwellers were hapless flies. I wished Papa hadn't mentioned the whistling as some of my old indignation returned.

'*Bonjour ma chérie!*' she smiled, and held out her arms: right, left, right!

'*Bonjour Madame.*'

'So, you're all alone my *cocotte*. Would you like to come downstairs?'

'No, no. I have to go and see a friend of my father's.'

'That's very good my little hen. If you need anything, just come and ask.'

'*Merci Madame.*'

I was a bit ungracious. What the hell. I whistled defiantly all the way up the stairs to our fourth floor apartment. My little hen indeed! Madame Nicole considered whistling to be very rude and badly brought up for a young girl. '*Les poules qui chantent, on leur coupe la tête.* Hens that sing have their heads chopped off.' Worse, she complained to my father that I was growing wild. I tried to whistle louder but couldn't.

Our flat on the fourth floor was very small. Two rooms made into one. A huge wardrobe in the hall which had to hold all our clothes, a comfortable kitchen in which we also ate and a bathroom. It was bright and sunny and full of character. My father's numerous books lined the walls, and the double bed, which also served as a sofa, was covered by one of my mother's many Cashmere shawls. There was a red and gold lacquered Chinese writing desk, mother of pearl encrusted Moorish chairs, golden Buddhas and other curios squeezed into available corners, shelves and furniture, and mystic paintings of sunset and storms on the Himalayan mountains adorned the walls. The last were with us only for safe keeping until they were moved to their final abode, the Nicholas Reorich Museum in New York. The flat had been a rare find, central, well appointed and ridiculously cheap. It was supposed to be temporary, but proved too convenient. It was much too small for all of us and so we were rarely together and in this way it exacted its own price. But then Paris too was to be for two years which were now nearing twenty.

My mother and father inhabited two different worlds from which each tried to glean meanings and treasures. My father looked for these in books, people, ideas, reflections, communication and the rich cultural life of the city. My mother's world was more tangible and located mostly in the *Marché aux Puces*, the flea market from where she would retrieve Thai Buddhas, Tibetan Thankas, Chinese carvings, Indian bronzes and, of course, the fabulous shawls from Kashmir.

Once she brought one back in its original 19th-century box: a slim rectangular cream box inscribed in gold *Châle des Indes*. Two flaps opened like double doors and in the yellowing tissue tied with a faded ribbon was the rich woven shawl. She explained that when she had married, among all the many saris and jewels, she had received but two small shawls. Like everything else, these were left behind in the partition and Cashmere shawls today were both expensive and rare, as they were no longer made. A large shawl could take a man a lifetime to weave. Many a man's sight and life had been lost in the making of these shawls. In the nineteenth century there had been a flourishing export trade to France. They were *à la mode* and every girl from a good bourgeois family was expected to have one in her dowry. The flea market was a veritable Aladdin's cave – full of shawls, all gradually finding their way into our small apartment. We slept over them and under them. Four trunks of shawls with a mattress over them made a bed, and my sister and I each slept on one of these. Shawls also served as blankets, as covers and my mother put them to their proper use by wearing them.

My father would continually polish his already excellent French so as not to miss its subtlest nuances, whereas my mother used her lack of it to her best advantage in striking

bargains. His concerns were about bringing the rich
wisdom of the East to the West, to build bridges, establish
dialogue and create synthesis. She was concerned with
retrieving the loot and returning it to where it rightfully
belonged and could be fully appreciated and valued. These
two very different worlds would meet in the flat. Papa
would discuss plans for the International Tolstoy and
Gandhi Conference to be held in Venice or Unesco's
Orient Occident cultural exchange programme of activities
sitting on a Cashmere shawl, as a still and silent gilded
Buddha looked into a sunset in the Tibetan Himalayas.
Names that I knew from book covers would be discussed or
sit in the room discussing. I would be set free and given
money to go off to the cinema. I saw *Ivanhoe* twelve times,
and knew it by heart.

My own little domain in the flat was the sideboard in the
kitchen. In it was stored what I had preserved of my books,
comics, film magazines and odds and ends. I looked
through them absently as I ate my sandwich, half thinking
what I might take to India if it came to the final packing.
Books in French, English, even German, a language I had
once known but since forgotten, like my own mother
tongue. *Li'l Abner*! I pulled it out and smiled. Yes! I'll go
and say hello or Hi, rather, to George Whitman. I hadn't
known which of my father's friends I'd intended to visit
when I'd spoken to Madame Nicole earlier, but now I
knew. George had given me *Li'l Abner* when I was eleven,
on hearing from my father that I was mad about comics. I
hadn't understood a word. I'd tell him that. He'd laugh.

I got off at St Michel and made my way to Le Mistral as
George's bookshop was called.

'It's not just a bookshop,' Papa explained to a friend as
we were driving there some time back, 'it's a most unusual
place. Quite unique. A club, a library all in one and more.
It's open till late, you can browse, borrow or buy. You can

sit and drink tea and chat, meet people. It's in the best
tradition of the Latin Quarter with American openness and
informality thrown in. George is a remarkable man.'

Unlike Madame Verlaine, George's descent from the
great poet Walt Whitman was an established fact. Le
Mistral was located in one of the oldest and most pictur-
esque parts of Paris close to the Cathedral of Notre Dame,
and the 12th-century church of St Julien le Pauvre. I
strolled in, browsed around for a while, and then went to
find George, looking the same as ever with his forked beard
and sharp eyes. He offered me tea and laughed heartily at
my news.

'You'll never leave Paris. No one ever leaves Paris. And if
ever they do they always come back.'

I sipped my tea and realized that George couldn't
possibly understand. He couldn't understand how far
India was, the problems of foreign exchange, the import-
ance of 'going home'. He had chosen to leave America. We
hadn't exactly chosen to leave India, or that it should be
partitioned.

The Cathedral looked down at me, silent, awe inspiring
and lit up to reveal its glory. As I looked at it I remembered
I hadn't told George about *L'il Abner*. Another time. I
walked through the Cité to catch the metro at Châtelet,
from where there was a direct line home. As I rode along I
thought more about home. Of course India was home:
ancient origins and ancestors, and at least I wouldn't have
to explain myself there! All those confusions: India was *Les
Indes*, the Indias. I couldn't be *Indienne* because I wasn't
from America, I was from India and therefore I was
Hindou. But no, I would explain, *Hindou* is used to define a
religious outlook and someone could be from India and be a
Christian, or a Muslim and therefore not be a *Hindou*.

'Ah, la la, this is too complicated.' Or there was: 'Which
India do you come from? English India, French India,

Portuguese India? . . . Indian India? Where is that?'

'People don't mean badly,' Papa would say. 'You must always be polite and patient.'

But Paris too is home, I thought as I entered the flat and looked around at its familiarity. I even know French better than any Indian language. It's the city of my childhood. Can I just lose it?

But then, my parents had lost the city of their childhood: Lahore.

I went to sleep with my confusion and awoke refreshed to another bright day. I told Marie Thérèse when she called that I proposed to spend the rest of my holiday visiting familiar parts of the city.

'That's a good idea. Where are you going today?'

'To Montmartre.'

Brought up as I was on the French *chansons*, and the singer poets, I quite naturally found myself singing 'Les Escaliers de la Butte' as I walked up the Rue St Vincent, where, according to the song, the poet met an unknown beggar girl, loved her, lost her and had composed this song that she may hear it at some street corner: 'Princess of the street, be welcome in my wounded heart.' The song always made me cry.

We'd come to Montmartre to buy cloth as there were some inexpensive by-the-yard shops. From quite a young age I was expected to take visitors from India shopping and sightseeing. But I put my foot down at the *Folies Bergères*. My parents were loath to go so the chore fell on me. It was the most boring place, but all the Indians felt they must visit it and when they did they looked thoroughly bored or embarrassed. After my second time, I demanded a raise in my pocket money.

*   *   *

On my return from Montmartre Rosine and I commiserated yet again over the Duchess.

'So if Maya means illusion and everything is illusion, then what is reality?' quizzed Rosine.

'I don't know. I can't remember. But *Moksha* I know means liberation.'

'Liberation? What's that?'

'I'm not sure. But it's important and that's what it's called.'

'Ah. *La philosophie indienne!*' She shrugged her shoulders. I did the same. We both laughed. The next morning, Jacques called to say that he had promised my father to look after me and he would take me to dinner, a worldly dinner, in a nice cute little club, *un petit club tout mignon*. I was to be ready and downstairs at eight.

I spent the day at L'Opéra, walking around to the tune of Yves Montand's song Place de l'Opéra, about the newspaper boy and the flower girl opposite with whom he is in love. I went into the shop where I would take visitors to buy French chiffon silk saris.

'Bonjour Mademoiselle. Ah but it's little Maya.' M. Jeannot embraced me. The mandatory three: right, left, right, and then asked the news of my mother and the family.

'Ah! if you go back to India you will have to come and buy lots of saris before you go. For your trousseau. Here I have something for you.' He returned with a chiffon scarf in graded shades of pink which he decided was 'perfect' and gift-wrapped it for me.

Back in the flat, I got out of my jeans and put on a sari. Jacques kissed my hand like a gallant, instead of the familiar three on the cheeks.

'Ah Maya, you are *élégante*. I am ashamed I asked you to

come down. I should have come with a bouquet to escort you.' He opened the car door. I blushed.

The club was small but chic and the centre cleared for a floor show. Our table was, well, fairly close to the empty space in which there was a deck chair and a basket. As we started our dinner the floor show started. A tall, well built blonde came on and to the sound of Peggy Lee's 'Fever': 'you give me fever', she danced her clothes off to cool in the heat of an imaginary sun.

'*Bon appétit*,' said Jacques with a highly amused smile.

'Is this supposed to give appetite?' I asked as the *danseuse* discarded her bra.

'Really Maya, you are so very English. It is worrying. But everything can change.'

A bit odd, I thought, sitting in a sari, talking in French and to be told I was very English of all things. 'I don't see why I am particularly more English than anything else,' I protested.

Jacques raised his hands in a gesture of mock despair. 'Exactly! That is *la tragédie!*'

'Do you bring Papa here?' I was taken aback by my tone.

Jacques laughed heartily. 'Certainly. But your papa my dear is a sage, *un philosophe*, he is on a different plane. But there is more to the world than philosophy! I told him I will look after Maya in my way. There is much to learn to become a woman.' He poured out some wine. The floor show ended, the lights dimmed and soft dance music filled the room. Well. This is Paris all right. Maybe not the Paris of my childhood, but still Paris.

'Now what would you say if I told you that the *danseuse* was not a woman?'

'Are you making fun of me or something?'

'*Allez* Maya. English again. Of course I am not making fun of you *ma chérie*. I am telling you the truth. It was not a woman, it was a man. It is true. Think about it.'

I admitted that there was something strange.

'Now a few years from now, you would be able to see that at once.' He winked.

'And that would be useful knowledge?'

'But of course. All observation is useful knowledge. And knowledge of good wine is culture.'

He filled my glass, which to my surprise was empty. Only Jacques could have brought me here. All my father's other friends were more serious, introvert, quiet. Jacques believed in the good life. I smiled. He was pleased.

'You can do the serious things with your father. Did he tell you about when he took me to see the new play by Beckett?'

I shook my head.

'Horrible. I mean, imagine going to the theatre to get depressed – ah! That is not for me! He tried to persuade me that the play was a brilliant *tour de force*, something new.' He shrugged his shoulders. 'I brought him here with me afterwards.'

I started to laugh. 'It's not very French to be anti-intellectual.'

'But it is very French to think for yourself. Chin!' He held up his glass. 'Remember that, and that you're a bit French too!' He winked and invited me to dance. Ah, yes, Paris, such delight.

The next few days songs guided my forays into the city. Walking down the Seine Yves Montand reminded me that all lovers needed for total happiness was a bit of sunshine, a walk along the river and a packet of chips. And the Seine herself, subject of so many songs: in one song she flowed to the first city, then rolled till the next and on reaching Paris she started to sing: *chante, chante chante chante chante le jour et la nuit*, sing day and night because the Seine was in love and her lover was Paris! '*Il n'y a plus d'après, à St Germain des Prés,*' sang Juliette Greco. 'There is no tomorrow at St Germain des Prés – there is only today.'

I cleaned the flat lovingly and with care, singing with the windows open. Accompanying the records of Juliette Greco, Charles Trenet, Yves Montand, Georges Brassens, Edith Piaf. Madame Nicole came up and joined me dancing in the flat, and we agreed with Edith Piaf that '*riche ou sans un sou, sans amour on est rien du tout.*' Ah songs! Edith Piaf! Jean Cocteau said that her death 'had made it impossible for him to breathe' and he himself died two hours later. That too was Paris.

On my last day I woke up early. Usually leaving didn't make much difference. It was part of my *habitude*. But this time I felt empty. No song came into my head. The clean flat looked wonderful. In a few years someone completely different might live in it. With what great philosophical concept could I make sense of my here and now? I looked around for clues. The gilded Thai Buddha smiled as always. Around me in the books and curios, I recognized the ways my parents had each tried to deal with their uprootedness and loss of home. I double checked Papa's list absently. Everything had been crossed off. I folded the paper. It had some writing on the back with a line through it. It was a poem he had been working on:

> We meet, we pass,
> We pause, or turn again,
> A moment stay, then blindly journey on.
> Little we know of others,
> Much of none,
> The secret self, in them,
> In us, unwon.

I folded the paper and put it in my pocket. It suited my melancholy. We would go, be forgotten and so be nameless and dead even if we were still alive.

Breakfast, I decided, was to be at Le Vigier.

'A hot chocolate and a croissant.' I gave my order to the waiter we had nicknamed the wolf because of his long sideburns. I looked vaguely into the street pondering over the great imponderables of existence: life, loneliness, death, forgetting, time . . . Rosine had not yet opened her shop. She rarely did before 10 a.m. Breakfast hubbed around me as orders were called out. Behind me, I heard the wolf's voice welcoming another customer. 'Bonjour Madame, it is some time since we have seen you.'

'Yes, I have been away,' came the reply. 'I have been to see my young cousin.'

'Is everything all right? Will you have the usual?'

'Yes. That's right. The usual. *Comme d'habitude.*'

I dipped my croissant into my chocolate and listened absently to the conversation behind me.

'Yes, I have been away to see a young cousin. She has become a nun.'

'Really!'

'Yes, they have a proper ceremony. She wears a ring on her wedding finger. They get married to Jesus you know. A proper wedding. A gold ring. So you could say that Jesus is now my cousin-in-law.'

My chocolate went down the wrong way and as I coughed I spilt some. Did I really hear that?

Who said it? I turned to see. It was the Duchess!

Incredible! I felt quite paralysed. Slowly I came to as the Duchess, now joined by a friend, was repeating her story. I asked for the bill and got up to leave. The Duchess looked up at me.

I passed her table and hesitated for a moment. '*Bonjour Madame Verlaine.*'

She raised her eyebrows in astonishment and then smiled. '*Bonjour Mademoiselle Maya.*'

My heart leaped and then pounded. I smiled and rushed out. I was walking on air. I was a cloud. In a daze. I floated up to the fourth floor, collected my small bag, and hugged Madame Nicole goodbye so tightly that she was startled.

Rosine was pushing up the grille as I called out to her.

'Rosine! Rosine! She's come back. She's there. *La Duchesse.*' Rosine looked across to the now empty table. 'I saw her. I spoke to her. She knows my name!' With a peal of laughter we fell into each other's arms.

'Have you got time for a coffee?'

I nodded.

She pulled down the grille and we walked across arm in arm to *Le Vigier*. 'She came back on my last day. I'm sure it's a sign. But of what?'

Rosine squeezed my arm. 'Of course it's a sign. It means that you will keep coming back to Paris, and also that wherever you are, you will always be a *Parisienne.*'

A song descended upon me: *La vie en Rose*, and it remained – throughout the train journey across France and over the sea.

Capitalism

JOE AMBROSE

Y ou can't blame buskers. Life itself is shabby and so are
buskers shabby. Don't call me prejudiced. I'm not
prejudiced at all. I love music, you see, I love it in all of its
forms. But there are two fat and dirty buskers who work the
underground and they must make more money than those
city gents busy collecting brain tumours, blood pressure,
plain old fashioned nervous breakdowns. They're typical
buskers, playing purist rockabilly for the joke rather than
the glory. They know nothing about the dignity of the
country man defending family, land, and religion. They
know about money and busking. I hate that shit.

None of this applied to him. He was foppish, reminiscent
of Jagger during his Hyde Park days. Lots of pastel silk
scarves. Black leather shirt. Old jeans. I mean I couldn't
keep my eyes off of him and that, to be sure, is a litmus test.
I like that concept. Life is a litmus test. You dip yoru wick
in the water and you see what happens. Life is a litmus test.

Now I'm not talking sex here. I'm talking showbiz. All
pop stars, you want to look at them. You even want to stare
at Barry Manilow, he's so fucking ugly. And you'd certainly want to look at, say, Elvis or Madonna. And if you
were normal and you were on the London Underground
and you came across this kid busking, you'd want to stop
and have a look. I travel a lot on the Central Line, getting
off at places like Oxford Circus and Tottenham Court
Road. It was principally on that line that I saw him

although sometimes he might be at work as far south as Green Park.

I guess the Central Line is a kind of sleazy place at the best of times. A sort of conduit bringing together happy shoppers, big shoppers, happy slaves, bookish types, fags on their way to toilets or fag cafés, heavy metal sluts on their way to clubs, tourists (especially tourists from my own country) wanting to spend money looking at manifestations of British imperialism. Me? I'm just from the Bronx and I got trapped here. This is not my country, my culture, and it is hardly my language. To some extent I'm a prisoner, I sometimes feel, or else a captive audience.

I mean the English they can hardly talk their own language anymore. I mean they can babble and communicate but they don't know the meaning of words or life. Naturally I have contempt. I come from a reasonably great country. I know culture. I couldn't stop looking at this pretty busker who played pretty good music, who turned out to be American too. But that is a long story and I can't handle long stories. I'm a product of the TV age and my attention span is limited – which is not to say that I lack understanding. I just have too much understanding and too much taste. I can read books as long as they're non-fiction and pretty good. I like to buy expensive magazines full of what they used to call New Journalism. Travel writing, interviews with boxers, investigative reports, getting Norman Mailer to talk to Clint Eastwood or getting an exposé on the New York boxing scene, I just love all of that stuff and will read it endlessly.

There was a time when I held a torch for Lou Reed. I used to think all kinds of credulous stuff about him. So when I heard the sexy busker playing *Sweet Jane* I was going to listen. I heard him before I saw him, before I came around the corner his guitar blared through a battery-operated practice amp. When I stood right in front of him staring I could hear his voice distinctly. It was a good voice, much better than his guitar playing, and he sounded deeply commercial. And he looked like some of the guys that I used to know when I was a kid. His hair was blond, didn't seem to be dyed, and he was seriously thin, like he never ate and lived on drugs. He smiled but not in a stupid servile busker way. He was not there to entertain the commuters but to entertain himself. End, in a sense, of story.

It goes without saying that I didn't stop to listen. You don't do that on the underground. You just keep going, tapping your newspaper against your hip, making it clear to anybody that notices you that you know the song. You try to get across the message that you have that song, in the original version on an original pressing, in your record collection. You try to give the impression that you're a bit of a collector. You direct a proprietorial look at anybody noticing you which seems to say 'That ain't a bad version. The kid got a little talent going down there.'

I did all of this and I also made eye contact with the busker. I like to think that that freaked him out just the slightest, making him think that I wanted to ramble around inside him, and yes I did. But inside his head, really, not inside those old stylish jeans. You can afford in this life, at this stage in our century, to leave that kind of shit to the freaks who like that kind of shit. Women are the worst offenders – women are like that all of the time. Faggots are worried about AIDS and have some, enforced, sense of decorum.

Anyway, even if he was just a bit freaked out, he quickly regained composure and nodded in my direction. So I fucked some money into his shoebox, nodded back at him, and went about my business. *That boy could go far*, I thought as I made my way by train to Notting Hill Gate, *that boy could become a wonder horse*. What I meant was, of course, a fucking stallion.

The next time he was off duty. I'd been up all night at an all-night party down near the Parliament. I found myself at dawn, little money and no plastic, heading south across Vauxhall Bridge, money for a night bus having been borrowed from a fellow reveller. It was really cold, not my kind of time or place, and I just wanted to be at home, drinking coffee and watching all-night television. The storage depots and the office blocks seemed to surround me and all the faces that passed me by seemed to be poor and hostile. Black kids on their way home from a House party hassled me, called me *Asshole* and *Fuckhead*. I don't really give a shit but it ain't good for morale.

And there was the busker coming towards me, heading north without guitar or songs. He looked so rich in his long coat that I was impressed all over again. Why did he busk when he had so much money and so much taste? He glanced at me, smiled, then speeded up as we drew closer. It was as if he expected me to grab him or throw him onto the ground or something. I toyed with the idea of asking for a fiver so I could hop into a taxi and rescue myself from that desperate part of town. But it was for the best to let him pass into the privacy and intimacy of the night. Within minutes I was rescued by a night bus in any case, and I forgot all about him for a while.

Until the next time, of course. Which was three days later under Tottenham Court Road in a tunnel, when he was busking again. I'd been working all morning and I was just a little stoned. I suppose that that made me cocky or something so I winked at him. He was singing a fucking Lloyd Cole song this time which didn't impress me at all. You know Lloyd Cole? Hopefully not – but that guy is just like everything that is wrong with the modern world. The song in question was that really bad one, the one about Eve Marie Saint in *On the Waterfront*, the best known of his fucking songs. But the kid looked better than ever. Every chick that passed him by was stopping to stare and cop a look. This was what sex was all about and he was dressed accordingly, combining the cool of our own bad times with the passion of the sixties and the wasted elegance of earlier times, maybe wartime.

So I dug into my pocket and found some pound coins for throwing into the shoebox and I started to tell him what I thought about Lloyd Cole while he was still singing.

'Yeah, I understand,' he said, working his way through an improbable guitar solo, 'I guess he sucks, and to somebody your age it's natural that he sucks. I think he sucks too, but you can't make a living doing Lou Reed and Iggy Pop all the time, man. Some of the time I have to do the Beach Boys, ya know what I mean? This is life, not fucking art. I want to make money and these are especially stupid representatives of the bourgeoisie.' And he began singing again, having explained himself to me in a neutral American accent that surprised me.

'Oк,'' I said, and went off about my business, such as it was.

I make money in strange ways. I prefer schemes and ruses to hard work and I do quite well. My wife is a very beautiful Japanese lady who looks like a Japanese Lauren Bacall. We get on really well and once a year she goes back to Tokyo with her sister. I rarely visit America and I have a good life, albeit an unconventional one.

This life of mine leads me down into the underground (I cannot drive a car but would travel by one if I could) and causes me to go from place to place, keeping appointments and striking small deals. I know the system well and I like it outside rush hours. So it didn't take me long to bump into the kid again. I was returning from a meeting that had gone badly. I had just been meeting with somebody who I thought was rich, with enough money for me to lay my hands on some of it, but who turned out to have no money at all. I was depressed and I felt that I was growing old, that I should stop trying to live on my wits and go for something reliable and rewarding. So it cheered me up no end to hear him singing Lou Reed just like the first time. It just made me feel better about the world. I walked over to him and started talking to him as if we were the very best of friends.

'I'll give you ten quid to come and have a cup of coffee with me,' was my rather silly suggestion.

'I'll make ten quid playing music here during the time it would take us to quit this station, find a coffee shop, find a place to sit, have our little chat, and get back to here again,' he said humorously enough.

'All right. I'll buy you a cup of coffee and give you no money. Just talk at ya.'

'That sounds better. Why don't we meet up in twenty minutes at the coffee bar over the Virgin Megastore on Oxford Street?'

I agreed to this, and headed in that general direction, while he got back to his work, playing something dreadful that was so dreary that I can never remember who wrote it or what its title is.

The Virgin Megastore coffee bar was more interesting than I'd expected it to be and I was impressed by his choice. I ordered two coffees and admired the waitresses while I waited for him. He arrived on time, just when I was getting bored with the bland pop-rock that was coming out of the speakers all over the complex. But that is the soundtrack of the modern world and you hear it everywhere. So we got to talking.

He was twenty although, as he pointed out, he looked a great deal younger. He told me that he came from rich San Francisco folks who disapproved of his promiscuity and constantly fought with him.

'My mother, she's just into her strict Catholic thing,' he explained, 'and she was always hearing these stories from her friends about how I was fucking their daughters and the whole thing just freaked my old man out. We were hurting each other so much that I just got to fuck out of there.'

He went to New York at first but moved to London, all the time reading, fucking, and listening to music. The usual writers – South Americans and Americans from the South. The usual women – schoolgirls and middle-aged married women. The usual music – American rock'n'roll and English punk rock. By the time that he arrived in London he'd realized that he was nothing special – he looked good but he had no other talent.

'I met up with this rich and elegant woman here in London,' he reminisced, 'and I had this affair with her. Maybe she thought that I loved her but I think she just liked being fucked. I think she's not a stupid woman. We are still friends and I still go see her, have some food, some of the time. But there was this businessman that she'd been hanging out with since she was a kid and – it seemed – she picked me up while they were fighting. When he came back to her she didn't want me around all the time. I was hip to that. I just went back to the busking. So what's the story?'

'What story?' I acted dumb, because he was staring right at me like we were at some high-powered business meeting.

'Are you a fag? That kind of story . . . you want to rescue me from a life of singing and set me up in a bedsitter somewhere because, if ya do, that'd be just fine with me.'

'Nah. I'm married.' Fucking Oscar Wilde was married, see where that got *him*.

'Married men get to be fags sometimes too.' The kid was a real liberal.

'I'm not a fag.'

'Coulda fooled me. Maybe you should take a long hard look at yourself.'

'Maybe I should take a long hard look at you.' It was mainly a word game and I was enjoying it. The nearest thing to a man that I'd ever fucked was a cheerleader from New Jersey.

'Yeah, well, I thought that was why we were drinking this coffee and being here in this place.' He was both amused and annoyed.

'You a prostitute? You consider yourself a prostitute?'

'Nah, I never did it with a man before.'

'And you want to do it with me now for money?'

'I'd do anything for money.' He was giving every restive appearance of being ready to go about his business. 'I'd even sing you a Leonard Cohen song for money. I'm a Reaganite American, man, and I believe in money more than anything. As for fucking, that's just something animals do and it don't interest me at all. I don't fuck, I make money and survive. And if you ever want to give me money you know where to find me. So long.'

With one flourish he smiled at me, picked up his guitar, stood up, and made his way to the exit. I noticed an old blue rinse and her daughter, at the next table, staring at me. I grinned at them and shrugged my shoulders. What a fucking guy!

The next day I was back on the Central Line and he was back at work. I passed him, winked at him, and was speeding up when I heard him shout after me: 'The next time, I'll buy you the coffee. How about it?' I turned, shrugged, and walked away. This is a fucking city and you meet all kinds of nuts around the place. You can't be too careful.

Paris-Michigan

SUSAN MONCUR

'Your mother did a *mean snake* dance,' my godmother Nancy told me once, and winked, as if that meant my mom was good in bed, then giggled, making a noise between a gurgle and a hee-haw, which wrinkled her nose, curled her upper lip to the tops of her gums and squeezed her eyes shut. Her head bobbed in counter-time to the hee-haws, she looked a little like a donkey. Then she gave me a demonstration, arms up framing her head, palms joined flat against each other, head jerking right and left, boom da da, boom da da – now she looked like an Egyptian. Then she collapsed on the couch giggling, she'd never been very good at it, not like my mom.

I remember a photograph I looked at often, fascinated, as a kid, finally 'stole' with a bunch more, took back to France like some kind of proof – showed my mom reclining in profile on a bearskin rug, peasant's skirt hiked up to mid-thigh, bare feet, slave bracelets around slim ankles, leaning back on her hands, face front, chin coy behind one nude shoulder, eyes smoldering into the camera lens, 'burning the film' maybe the photographer had said. My dad? Or Nancy. Her and my mom were best friends.

'Nancy-Pancy still has those legs,' I say to no one while watching the video of my sister Lily's wedding for the second time. 'Beauty contest legs', I say, and giggle. Second time I'm starting to notice things. First time I was too keyed up, although don't ask me why I procrastinated

six months before getting around to watching it, or trying
to. I was told it would cost two hundred francs per minute
of film to make a French cassette out of my American one
because French and American video systems are different
and never the twain shall meet. Par for the course I thought.
Did I expect anything 'family' to just fit after so long? Ten
times more expensive, if not twenty, than plane tickets to
Michigan for me, Franck and Davie, which is why we
didn't go to the wedding in the first place! Could have gone
by myself but I knew Franck and Davie wanted to go as
much as I did. I could have given my mom and sister the
choice of one out of three but that would have been a little
perverse.

Two days ago I got lucky, found someone with a three-
in-one-tri-standard video recorder, even more than I
needed. So here I am, enjoying progress. The guy whose
apartment I'm in, another exiled American – 'exiled'
sounds so serious, it's not like the States are difficult to
leave and come back to unless your underwear, or your
intestines, God forbid, are full of drugs – says I can watch it
as many times as I want. He's been away longer than me in
fact. Except after thirty years maybe you aren't away
anymore; you live somewhere else.

There goes my brother Billy in a blue suit and tennis
shoes, setting off firecrackers in the field. Him and his
girlfriend came up from Houston. Someone not on camera
keeps saying:

'They're gonna come ride *at* 's, jus' wait 'n' see ...
they're gonna come ride *at* 's ...', mouth full of jelly
donuts. I'm too far away to throw stones I guess but still,
why don't they pronounce their words! Should hear themselves with my foreign ears once.

Mom's new kitchen looks spacious. Haven't been to this
house. Pine panelling, rosebushes on the wallpaper. Recognize a magazine next to the sink, some pictures of me inside,

must have shown it around. I *hate* that. Can see her flipping through pages, where is she, where *is* she, *here* she is, my daughter the model, who didn't care enough about us to be here today. Which isn't true but someone might think it. I thought it. Whew! I can hear the guests thinking questions they don't dare ask, like: don't models make enough money to travel? Well, Mom'd probably say, you'd never know from looking at me but she's no spring chicken! You have to be younger than a spring chicken to get into most of those magazines. Or for sure they were dying to ask: does she do nudes? One thousand nosey questions in one.

'Here we are wit' all de chow . . .' *the* chow, *the* chow – woman caterer, cateress? says to the camera, bending over a big table, placing bowls of food, saran-wrapped, see it shining, for after the ceremony. 'What are you filming?' she says, discovering the camera has semi-circled behind her.

'I'm not filming *that*,' says the invisible cameraman. She thinks her butt's being zoomed in on, bending over the bowls, which it is.

There's Nancy again, with Sam, my godfather, a Frank Sinatra look-alike, and Steve and Susie, Lily's godparents, and Mitch, an old friend of Dad's. Dad hasn't seen any of this crowd, the ones he knows, since he left Mom, whole first part of his life, and mine. Lily's hadn't even begun.

Here they come. Tears spring to my eyes like they'd been eyedroppered in, dammit, even the second time I watch – Lily on our father's arm, picking up her feet carefully in high white heels, long fancy dress, veiled face . . .

'She's *beau*tiful . . .' I lip-read a woman saying to Mom who moves away from her, wants to follow their passage in peace. Still twenty yards away under the trees father and daughter start walking slowly in time to the music, Vivaldi maybe, like a lullaby, like they hadn't decided, take your time, little sister, slow as you can, never again, this, perfect, squeeze it, milk it, right step, feet together, left step, feet

together, back and forth, forward, rocking, Daddy's finally
rocking you, ... caring for you here, tense and teary,
stranger's bed, sheets smell musty, impotently muttering
to myself, you and your guests, as if all this hadn't already
happened ... her corsage is trembling, she's sobbing.

I had a chance to leave, that's all. Never thought I'd stay
away, they'd never visit, like Mars for them here. In fact,
isn't as easy to come and go as I said, always forget, pain,
pleasure, 'til bang! hits you on the head. Percentage of
people who jet around the world making it small is still
small enough, so Mom who's never been on a plane is in a
definite majority. Oh I miss them all right. I decide things,
need something to think, no one's here to talk to, if there
was I might not dare. Maybe what I decide's a fairy tale. Do
they decide things? probably don't feel the need, life's more
linear. Doesn't mean they don't change, I see it, watching
them live from my other planet, palpable change since the
last time I touched them. Need a spare heart to feel what I
feel, like breaking the screen, scooping out and encircling,
bear-hugging, twenty years of marriages, birthdays, births
and deaths, helping hands, mine and theirs, knowing what
they'll say before they say it, except now I'd probably get it
wrong. Is the missing I feel like mourning? Do I mourn
them?

The son was called prodigal (was the daughter called
loose?), can't ask them if they miss me. The one who leaves
is the one who returns, finds the ticket money, at least the
tri-standard, re-adapts to them, having adapted to others,
neither here nor there, nor a country of one.

I think they're afraid of change. They'd like to visit but
they'd be faced with their fear and have to ask themselves
what they're so afraid of – understanding why I left? Didn't
know I was leaving. Stayed away then; feeling the fear they
think I felt. Maybe I did. Maybe I was fleeing their fear.
Maybe these thoughts for them are foreign as French.

The priest monologues on, moralizing, familiar, stage whispers. When he says: 'Let us look at our sins and selfishness...' I turn off the sound, wishing I could keep on the crickets, and watch Lily listening, the Queen of her Day.

From my bedroom loggia, I hear a voice downstairs telling the middle of a story: '... Then one night a woman came up to me, you're Jack Jaynes, aren't you. You don't know me, but I know someone *you* know *very well*. I didn't say anything. I said oh yes oh yes oh yes ...' Church bells start ringing in the city, or a recording of church bells. Lily discreetly wipes her eyes. Tears fill mine in dumb imitation. Where am I? The sun is shining kitty-corner onto the television screen, across which, I don't find it as strange as I could, my family members are moving in miniature. I haven't been introduced to the reminiscing Americans downstairs, an artist's atelier in the fourteenth district, Paris, France, a winter afternoon in 1992. It's raining on my sister's wedding tent in a medium-sized town in Michigan, summer 1991, and the raincloud light through the tent walls makes her guests' faces orange.

'I would like to introduce you to a new couple, Mark and Lily, and I think they deserve a hand...' the priest says as I turn the sound back on. I self-consciously applaud with the sunset-colored congregation, in two seasons and landscapes at once.

'Freezing' for pictures. Two women who've just met, arms around each other's waists, posing, the mothers. Can't see the photographer, probably Mom's husband Mal. He must be using high-speed film which admits movement on a rainy day, but wedding guests just naturally 'freeze' for posterity. Much of the video now will be filming the picture-taking. Stand up straight Mom. Give us a little

snake dance – boom da da, boom da da ... wonder if she
drinks? She's let her hair go all white, looks good with her
white satin suit, 'Parisian' cut, tiny crystal beading on the
front of the jacket. The other mother's in blue ruffles. Mom
wins. She so seldom makes the effort, I'd forgotten how
good she looks when she does. Hasn't seen Dad in thirty
years! Why she made the effort. He looks like he must have
had a face-lift, hairline hardly receded, sixty-six years old,
could pass for fifty. Photogenic. I take after him. Lucky me.
    Lily joins the moms. Everyone smiles obediently. My
antique earrings and brooch would have been picture-
perfect on her Russian doll's dress but I sent them too late.
That's the unchanging part of the story, the procrastinating
part, my personal 'freezing', psychological slow-motion.
Now the groom's playboy father joins Lily and the
mothers. Looks like he practices some of his moves in front
of the mirror. False-tooth smile, or just false, sandy hair,
mustache, suit, shirt, shoes. Imagine the time he spent
shopping for exactly the right beige. Now Lily's new
husband, also sandy good-looking; he works for Ford. Now
the Air Force officer brother, so handsome in dress
uniform, blood-red cummerbund peeking passionately
out of a white spencer jacket that shows off his rear;
wasn't eligible for combat in the Gulf war. Looks eligible
to me. Now giant and gangly brother Billy; 'say
"cheeeeeeeeeese"' ... someone in there's saying
'sheeeeeeeeiiiiiiit' ... Mom still points at things then lets
her hand drop like a dead weight, slapping and bouncing
off her thigh, bam ba ba boom da. Still swings her hips
easily, even in a sophisticated satin suit. Used to shimmy
around the kitchen when I was little, embarrass me. Still
looks more black than white when she laughs, when she
moves, except her shoulders slope, so do mine and Lily's,
round and defensive, head like a turtle's, wants to disappear
inside somewhere, shell of her breast. It's as if you can see

from the outside, blood doesn't run freely on top. Although I'll bet her swinging hips keep her tight top looser than it'd like, force her shoulders to move, it's all attached. Your man-catching, baby-making, shimmy hips keep your heart pumping on time, in tempo, boom, bam, boom, boom, *swing* wise fleshy hips, jiggle her chin up, get her eyes off the ground, she's not dead yet.

Lily lifts her skirts to remove her lacy garter. Someone starts boom-bamming the Stripper Song and she finishes the ritual like a professional. Arm swings round and round, garter flies blind, the Air Force officer jumps and grabs, misses but doesn't give up, scurries after it in the grass with athlete's reflexes, almost knocks down the cameraman, the whole scene wobbles, scene in a movie: Family Social Studies. Who got the bouquet? the flower girl, officer's slipping the garter up her young leg. Could have been my young leg.

My curiosity isn't satisfied with the bad definition in a video film. There's less lines than in a face. Mom's sad eyes used to make me uneasy, I think they still do, but I can't really see her, even close-up. It's her I keep watching like a laboratory specimen, ready for anything. Photographers used to ask me why did I look sad. 'I'm not sad!' I'd say before I learned how to cheat on my expressions, smolder into the lens. Even sitting down, Mom's shoulders look tense, or deliberately hunched; if she ever lets go her arms will fall out of their sockets. Her neck must get stiff, mine does. What's she trying not to feel, squeezing up like that? Maybe she's just afraid of being taken by surprise. Easier to see her from a distance though, in a film I can put back in the box. How many distances does that make? miles, years, experiences, language: '*Maman! est-ce que je te manque?!*' Paranoia because of all the former – we haven't talked in so long, the distances seem greater than the nearness ever was; where would we begin? And now I have the wedding video.

They've always had my magazine pages to show and put
back in the drawer. 'Mom', that's easiest, with an American
accent. Sounds normal when Lily says it in the video:

'Mom? come 'ere for pictures, Mom.'

I asked for a map in a Niagara Falls drugstore, five years
ago, when Franck and I went to the States to get married,
spur of the moment, only known each other six months.
Mom got all strange, almost refused to function the first
few days, couldn't understand why I'd come, what I
wanted after so long. I'd been in and out of one marriage
without her, why was I obliging her to do it with me the
second time? Things happen Mom, what can I tell you?
Whether you're ready for them or not. Ready or not, here I
come – so I asked for a map and got sent to the brooms and
mops. I asked twice and twice got sent to the brooms and
mops before figuring out I say 'map' like they say 'mop',
now how can I have been ready for that? Evidence of my
foreignness in a drugstore while I was feeling right at home.
And I bet I say 'Mom' like 'Mum'.

'You talk funny,' Lily said, one of my first visits, she was a
second grader. I don't hear myself with American ears, not
from not listening, but certain things, maybe I don't want to
know, even me who thinks she wants to know everything.

One of the nice things about living so far from where you
came is you forget you have a family, unless you're
reminded by a marriage, a birth, a death. It's a little like
you'd been conceived at eighteen, or whatever age you left,
especially after twenty years, and five, six visits. And
whatever you've done, you've done, your self-conceived
self. Which is completely untrue but a nice thought. Nice
feeling too.

I got a letter from my mom this morning, telling me my
godmother Nancy's mother died, asking me to send my
condolences, saying she'd write soon, as if what she sent
wasn't writing, just news and duty.

My sister is so gracious in her gown. I suppose I was
afraid of feeling betrayed, watching the big wedding I
never had. But I was never there to have it. And it was fine,
I mean, if anything, I feel like the betrayer, like I should
have visited more often, sent berets, Arpège, cheese plates,
written and phoned more – I haven't shared much of my
so-called glamorous life. Was it? I was too busy, didn't
want them to think I was showing off, although that's
exactly what I did every time I visited. My brother Billy
once, a long time ago, before he moved to Houston but he
already thought like Houston, called me a pretentious
bitch, and the only reason I said I liked Detroit was I lived
in Paris, not with the niggers like he did. I said not only did
I live with them, I'd slept with a few. We didn't have to
think like the neighborhood we were brought up in, did
we? His face froze, until he could hide whatever he was
feeling in an expression, which turned out to be a crooked
smile:

'Oh the girls in France, walk around without no pants
. . .' he sang to me mockingly, doing a little hula dance.

Got a little headache from the long-distance participa-
tion, trying so hard to see more lines than there were, trying
to see everything I missed, head feels big and square as a TV
set. Guess that's a small price for being there. I swear at
times I saw myself, my empty space under the tent. In fact
at this very moment I feel *split* right down the middle,
Franco/American and never the twain shall meet! Can't be
in two places at once.

Maybe it's easier to be in *five* places at once. I've always
wanted to live in Rome, in London, on a lake in Norway.
I've got a girlfriend who has a house on a lake in Norway.
There you go, showin' off again Frenchie, Billy'd say. Billy,
listen to me: I want every person I meet, every home, hotel,
city, country, I visit or live in, to leave a mark on me. I want
to know why I grow old. If I could I'd become each race in

turn, see what each color feels like: black, brown, yellow, red, man, beast, river, tree, am I going too far Billy? Good. Don't you ever suspect whole worlds the other side of those all-weather blinders you're obliged to wear to stay comfortable in your poor white hole of an attitude? Or have you forgotten you're wearing them? I know what you're going to say and I'll bet I get it right. *I'm* the poor white who couldn't afford to come to her sister's wedding. You got me there Billy, but listen – families leave such big marks, by their presence, by their absence, they start out with such an advantage over us. If we want to see and understand anything without them, other than them, it's never too soon to start; or too late; I can't stop now. The world's so big and varied, *Billy*, aren't you afraid of missing things?! Even if we never stop trying we're going to miss most of it. That thought makes me crazy. What makes you crazy, Billy?

Litany for
the Homeland

JANETTE TURNER HOSPITAL

A supernova is on its way, it is even now shopping through the galaxies of which there are millions upon millions, its arrival in our neighbourhood – so astronomers tell us – is long overdue, it is casually browsing in the Milky Way, entirely neutral, without malice or forethought of any kind, and it could drop in on us.

On earth, our homeland.

On *Terra Australis*, on Queensland, on Brisbane, on Newmarket Road, Newmarket, on the wooden house with its high ant-capped stilts and on the mango tree and on the spot below the frangipanis where I first made intimate contact with the heavenly hosts. This was a miracle. I was looking through my father's telescope and gobbling light years like water.

Under the frangipani tree at the age of seven, lost, homesick for Melbourne which had so recently been mislaid, bemused by the fact that I could clearly see the craters on the moon but not the beloved grandparents left behind, homesick under the frangipani and the Queensland sky, I collided with immensity, outer and inner, and with the great riddle of our foothold on the whirligig of space.

A supernova is on its way and it could drop in on us.

We take it personally.

Among the galaxies, we are not city folk. Earth itself, *this goodly frame ... this most excellent canopy, the air, look you, this brave o'erhanging firmament, this majestical roof fretted with golden fire*, why, it has been demoted since Copernicus and Kepler to the outer bush-league suburbs of the cosmos, our sun itself just a boondocks firecracker, our whole solar system some 30000 light years from the core of the universe. We are galactic hillbillies. *Beyond the black stump* is our address. The refulgent snuffing out of our entire planet, homeland of billions, would be nothing more than a third-rate piss-ordinary common little matchflare of a nova just one galaxy over, and we know it. Yet we place ourselves front and centre. Still the galaxies wheel around the hub of our own buzzing heads. This is home, we presume to say with touching and ridiculous hubris, sticking a pin into a spinning ball in the margin of the margins of the void.

In margins and in longings: this is where all homelands begin.

Once upon a time a mapmaker doodled in the edges of his maps, and wished a place into being and dreamed up 'The Arguments for the Existence of Terra Australis, 1764': *Having shewn that there is a seeming necessity for a Southern Continent to maintain a conformity in the two hemispheres, it rests to shew, from the nature of the winds in the South Pacifick Ocean, that there must be a Continent on the South.*

And so there was.

Captain Cook, with sextant and compass, bumped into it and traced its bumps onto paper.

Yet homeland exists before and after maps. The Great Unknown South Land, wished onto the blank spaces of cartographers' knowledge, was already home to Sam Woolagoodjah's people:

> *The first ones, those days,*
> *shifted from place to place,*
> *In dreamtime before the floods came.*

We, the visitors, all of us, those who came in 1788 and those who came later and those who came last year, we the visitors acknowledge the presence of the first ones brooding over and under and before and after all our maps, those first ones who are still with us in the land, all of us together in the margins of the Milky Way, all of us passing through, both latecomers and first ones, those Wandjinas, *bird Wandjinas, crab Wandjinas . . . She the rock python. He the kangaroo*, all those ancient ones on whose flesh and river-veins we latecomers have so recently presumed to tread, to set up camp, to speak of home.

Have mercy upon us for we have been crude and arrogant guests and have given much offence.

Have mercy upon us.

> *Now you see nothing is made up,*
> *Each father has been told what happened:*
> *How Wandjina Namaaraalee made it all*
> *How he sent the flood*
> *How he said no.*

First ones and visitors, we shift from place to place, we build homes, we construct a homeland, we deconstruct it, we make and unmake, we wander from past to future *for here we have no continuing city but we seek one to come*, we wait together for the bush fires, the floods, the wars, the supernova, the millennium, the Second Coming, for Wandjina Namaaraalee to send again the great deluge that will sweep us back to the Dreaming where the first ones are, *world without end, amen.*

And it came to pass in those days, the days of childhood under the mango and the frangipani trees, that a wild boy beckoned from the back fence to the girl with the telescope.

The fence was soft and rotten and choked with passionfruit and crucifix orchids, and the boy pushed his head and shoulders between the palings and crooked his index finger. He had glittering eyes.

Beyond the fence was paddock. In the middle, where footballers trampled Saturdays and Sundays into dust, the paddock clung to its legal but provisional state; its thick margins had already slid back under bush. Unnameable acts, thrilling, dangerous, illicit, were said to take place under cover of tea-tree scrub, even during daytime, even during soccer games, even Sundays. Secrets bred there like rabbits. When the girl with the telescope put her ear against the fence palings, she could sometimes hear a murmur of voices and low throaty laughter, and the rustle of all that was forbidden. The bush pressed up against the fence, forever threatening to cross the line, forever sucking the backyard out between the palings.

'Come into the paddock,' the boy enticed. 'Come and play with me.'

'I'm not allowed.' The girl with the telescope recognized the boy. She knew him from school. He was utterly disreputable, he was caned every single day, *but he doesn't feel a thing* ran the playground legend, because the boy always grinned, jaunty, when he came back from the headmaster's office. It was said that he tamed flying foxes and kept them as pets, it was said that he could fly, it was said that he could travel underground and pass through walls and that he had a magic protector, a guardian angel maybe, or maybe a devil, who held an invisible shield between his backside and the cane. He was bad. All the teachers and all the girls said he was bad. His name was Paddy McGee.

Paddy-with-his-head-between-the-palings laughed. It was a low, wicked, irresistible sound. His glittering eyes pulled at the girl. 'What's yer name?' he demanded.

The girl searched for a name. 'Stella,' she said at last,

because she had the stars at her fingertips and she had been studying maps of the sky and she was someone else now, not the girl she had been in Ballarat where her grandfather had pointed out the planets and named them, and not the girl she had been in Melbourne, and she certainly didn't want to be the girl she was at her new Brisbane school. She was reinventing herself.

'No it's not,' the boy said. 'You're new. Where're ya from?'

'I'm Stella,' she said stubbornly. 'I'm from the moon. You wanna look?'

The boy smiled his dangerous smile and she smiled back (she knew she had crossed a line), and he wriggled through the fence and joined her under the frangipani tree and she held the telescope for him. He was filthy, he gave off a musky bush smell, and where his hand touched her arm it burned her in a damp feverish way.

'Can't see anything,' he said.

She turned the focusing ring with trembling fingers. 'You will,' she promised. 'You have to get it focused right. Tell me when.'

'Holy Jeez!' he said. 'Struth!' Every word could attract a bolt of lightning from God, yet he lived, he breathed, he laughed his wicked and jaunty laugh, he was a miracle of fearlessness.

'What can you see?' she asked.

'Craters and stuff, holy Jeez!' He laughed in a breathless excited way and turned on her his glittering burning eyes. 'Hey,' he said. 'You're OK for a sheila. You got guts.'

At school, he meant. The taunting, he meant, and the other stuff, the bullying. She didn't think she had guts at all, she was terrified.

'I go for guts,' Paddy McGee announced, placing the telescope down in the thick unmowed grass. 'I came lookin' for ya. I followed ya home.'

She knew this meant she was marked, just as he was. She knew this meant he recognized the mark on her, and that it was somehow visible to everyone at school.

Through the open neck of his shirt, she could see the dirty silk cord around his neck and the gold chain and the delicate little gold cross. 'What's that?' she asked, touching the cord with an index finger.

'It's me scapular.' He took hold of her wrist and licked her finger with his tongue. 'Come into the paddock,' he said. 'There's some good trees to climb. You wanna catch tadpoles with me at Breakfast Creek?'

'Yeah,' she said, 'I reckon.' And recklessly, heedlessly, she went. She climbed through the fence with the boy who was half-wild and only half-tamed, and crossed into no-man's-land, and that was where she sensed she belonged.

Something there is that doesn't love a boundary line. In the medieval *Books of Hours*, people step out of goldleaf miniatures and into the margins and sometimes right off the page. Falcons and hounds and pheasants and antlered deer, marginal to the Holy Offices for the day, outside the pale of theology, persist in nosing their way in from the white edges of the page to the text. And in response, as though lured by the exuberant outsiders, words put forth glowing tendrils, curlicues of *Dominus*, fronds of P and W and T which finger their way past the borders, past the rapture of martyred saints, into the white parchment margins where they swell and turn into gryphons, dragons, creatures of glowing crimson and lapis lazuli that are neither fish nor fowl, text nor subtext, not fully on this page and not quite on the next.

These are my kin. They are always beckoning me to the mysterious space behind the word, between the pages, beyond the pale and the fence palings and the text and the sanctioned structures. Their eyes glitter. Listen, they murmur seductively: rules are for transgressing, borders for crossing. They whisper: no little man from Customs and Immigration stands at the doors of memory or imagination demanding to see your passport. No arts bureaucrat or ComLit satrap can stamp *OzLit*, *CanLit*, *FemLit*, *MigrantLit*, or *Displaced Person* on your visa. Censors and critics alike overlook the margins. In the margins one is ignored, but one is free.

That is where homeland is.

In that shifting space, kinfolk know one another by secret signs; and wherever kinfolk meet, homeland soil coalesces about their feet in the mysterious way that coral cays, like seabirds pausing in flight, anchor themselves to the Barrier Reef.

Down by Breakfast Creek where the warm water sucks at mangrove roots, Paddy McGee shows the houseboat where he lives. It doesn't look like a house, and it doesn't look like a boat. Stella is round-eyed with disbelief and an excitement she cannot quite name. To live in a creek, to live in something that can move away, to live, in a sense, *nowhere*, it suggests that seemingly immutable laws can be called into question.

'But you can't *live* in a creek,' she says, tugged at by the rules, by what is known and what is allowed.

'Why not?'

And she looks down a mirrored corridor of *why nots?* infinitely multiplying themselves and leading to who knew what possibilities.

'Because.' She says it lamely, not really resisting, more than willing to be swept into a world where houses swim. 'What's your address, then?'

'Breakfast Creek.'

Paddy McGee, Breakfast Creek, Brisbane. Stella Maris, Crater Lane, The Moon. She smiles to herself, and Paddy McGee laughs, complicit.

Sometimes (so he says) his Mum and Dad are there (though Stella never sees them), sometimes not. His Dad is mostly at the pub or the races, he says; his Mum is a barmaid at the Newmarket Pub. Most days he comes to school, but often not. On the days when he doesn't go to school, she knows he will be waiting for her at the back fence, beckoning, and she will wriggle out between the palings into the forbidden world of bush and creek.

'Oh,' she says vaguely when asked, 'I was up in the mango tree reading a book.' She is famous, both at home and at school, for disappearing and for reading books.

Paddy McGee never reads books, but he knows more than anyone she has ever met. He knows the saps of trees and their differing uses, he knows where tadpoles breed, he knows which ants bite and which don't, he knows how to read the telltale flying-fox tracks in banana clumps.

At school, he knows nothing.

At school, Paddy McGee and the girl live on different planets and it would be quite impossible for them to speak or to acknowledge each other in any way. They are absolute strangers at school, they never even look at each other. Nevertheless she is always conscious of him. Once, in the playground mêlée (she does not hear or feel these things any more, she goes away to another place inside her head, and it is said of her, as it is said of Paddy McGee, that she is made of wood, that you can kick her and she won't feel a thing, and in fact this has become true; there's a trick she has learned); but during one of these times when things are happening and she is somewhere else, inattentive, she does become aware of Paddy tossing punches around and screaming *Leave her alone, you bloody bullies, leave her alone!*

He is caned for this violent behaviour.

On another occasion, for reasons unclear, one of the teachers, a rough giant of a man named Mr Brady, thrashes Paddy McGee to within an inch of his life, and the hushed class watches in fascinated terror as blood oozes from the purple welts on Paddy's legs. The classroom building is high up, on stilts above the cool under-the-school where the children eat lunch, and Mr Brady, convulsed by some inner cyclone of rage, finally throws the cane across the room (it cuts inadequate to his fury), and picks Paddy McGee up by the shoulders ... Paddy McGee being small and wiry, though *tough as bootleather*, teachers say. Mr Brady shakes Paddy McGee as though he were a stray tomcat and he holds him out the casement window.

'I'll teach you, you insolent filthy little mick,' thunders Mr Brady.

A number of the girls in the class are crying with fright. Stella herself has moved right into Paddy McGee's body, she can feel Mr Brady's claws eating into his flesh, she can feel the sickening air below his dangling feet, she can feel the warm trickle when he wets his pants. Perhaps the still eye of his own storm reaches Mr Brady, or perhaps he hears the nervous shuffling of feet and the murmurs and the crying of girls. Quite suddenly he stops. He goes slack, as though the storm has exhausted him. He drags Paddy McGee back through the window and dumps him on the floor like a sack of sugarcane cuttings and orders gruffly, 'Get back to your seat.'

It is the only time in recorded history that Paddy McGee is unable to flash his jaunty smile at the class, but he most certainly does not cry and he does not speak. In spite of the wet stain on his khaki shorts, he fixes his glittering eyes on Mr Brady and he stands as tall as his purple-striped legs and drenched pants will permit. The class is as one person, scarcely breathing. It seems to the class that something curious is happening now, that one end of an invisible seesaw is going down and the other end, the Paddy McGee end, is going up. A whiteness has appeared around Mr Brady's lips. No one moves, no one breathes. Then Paddy McGee turns and walks from the classroom, head high. He never comes back.

That afternoon he does not appear at the back fence, but when Stella slips through the palings and through the bush and across the paddock, she finds him down by the creek. They sit side by side, saying nothing.

At last Paddy McGee says, 'You wanna be my blood sister?'

'Yes,' she says.

And with his pocketknife, he makes a small cut in the vein at his wrist, and then in hers, and he places his wrist against hers, flesh to flesh, blood to blood.

She never sees him again. He vanishes. Day after day, she waits for him to come to the back fence, she roams the creek, but the houseboat has gone without a trace. Weeks go by. She begins to fear she dreamed up both the houseboat and Paddy McGee, but then Mr Brady makes a terse announcement. 'Good riddance,' he says. 'Bad blood.'

And she is comforted. She is comforted by the fact that Mr Brady *had* to say his name, and by the precious drop of Paddy McGee's bad blood in her veins.

Who decides what is margin and what is text? Who decides where the borders of the homeland run? Absences and silences are potent. It is the eloquent margins which frame the official history of the land. As for geography, there are divisions and boundary lines that fissure any state more deeply than the moat it digs around its nationhood.

In every country there are gaping holes. People fall

through them and disappear. Yet on every side there are also doors to a wider place, a covert geography under sleep where all the waters meet.

From time to time, when I am least expecting it, in the most unlikely countries, I run into Paddy McGee. He wears unpredictable names but I always recognize him by his eyes and by the mark of the outcast on his forehead. Like some ancient but ageless mariner, he keeps seeking me out to finish his tale, he keeps setting his compass for my shores. And whenever I see him, I find I have the mud of a Queensland creekbed under my feet.

In Boston his name was Franklin D. He was one of my students at MIT, though he was a good bit older than the others. He wore jungle-camouflage combat fatigues with the Marines insignia removed. I never saw him in anything else, nor did I ever see him without his rollerblades on. They seemed attached to his feet like calluses and he moved on them with dazzling speed and grace and dexterity, his feats eyecatching and incredible. He could skate up flights of stairs and down them. He moved along the endless corridors of MIT, especially the famous Infinity Corridor, head and shoulders above crowding students and professors, weaving, braking and pirouetting, swooping along like some exotic jungle creature, part human, part bird. Certainly flamboyant. He skated down subway entrances, into trains, onto buses, into bars, and into class. I think the desire to be untrammelled had blazed its own evolutionary detour and caused his legs to sprout wheels. He was doing a Physics degree on the Veterans' bill. He was black.

In my office, we were discussing the profoundly disturbing stories he had submitted: tales of gang rape as weekend sport, casual deaths, violent excitements.

'I don't know how to grade these,' I told him. 'I can hardly bear to read them. They frighten me.'

It was as though I had turned a key, as though all his life he had been waiting for someone to acknowledge: your life is frightening.

'I'll tell you two stories,' he said.

His first death: he was six years old, a basketball-obsessed street kid in Harlem playing on a charred lot between stripped cars when he saw two teenage boys knife an old man for his cash. The man struggled. 'Forget it, Gran'pa,' the boys said, and slashed him several times across the chest. Grandpa's chest unfurled itself slowly toward the child Franklin D. like a fresh steak, and Grandpa looked at his own ribs in mild surprise and raised his gnarled hands vaguely to hold himself in before he curled forward like the steak of his chest and died on the sidewalk. This happened in slow motion, Franklin D. said. It took an extraordinarily long time for Grandpa to hit the ground. Franklin D. felt nothing at all, he said. Nothing at all. Except that suddenly he had to run inside to the bathroom and vomit.

A story about the Marines: when he turned eighteen, Franklin D. signed up because it was a job, the only one he could get. He was promised good pay, a uniform, status, women, the chance to become a finely tooled killing machine, an adventure to remember. He remembered, constantly, another Marine in the same company. What this other Marine used to do for a hobby on afternoons off, was to catch a squirrel or a chipmunk and skin it alive so delicately, so tenderly, with such a sharp and masterly knife, that the animal still lived and trembled in the palm of the craftsman's hand after it was totally skinned. Then the Marine would let it go.

'A thing people don't understand about the Marines,' Franklin D. said, 'is that once you've signed up, you realize in the very first week you want out, but you've got six years like a Mack truck in front of you. I've known guys,' he said, 'break their own legs to get out of combat drill. The problem with being in the Marines,' he said, 'is figuring out how to become a human being again when you get out. When you get out,' he said, 'the only people you can talk to are war vets and other ex-Marines. You're not army, you don't know how to think civilian, you're *nowhere*.'

'But what do you do with all the stuff in *here*?' he demanded, knocking on his forehead. 'You need a garbage truck to cart it away. If I could write stories and send them to you . . .' he said. He held his head in his hands as though the clamour inside was deafening. 'If I could let it *out*,' he said. 'If I could send you letters.'

He did. He still does. With Franklin D., I slipped through fence palings at MIT and went to bars in Cambridge and Boston I would have been afraid to visit alone (me and Franklin D. and his rollerblades). I thought he knew more than most people at MIT. I thought he had the dignity of Paddy McGee. He spoke of Harlem, I spoke of Queensland . . . not such different places.

In northern Manitoba, Paddy McGee had a Cree name, and he surfaced in a ramshackle van at a tiny airport, 54°N. (I was on a reading tour of prairie outposts, heading north to the tundra.) The drive into town was long enough for two entire life histories to be exchanged, though it seemed to me that the bridge which divides strangers from kin had been crossed (in the mysterious way in which such things happen) before we got out of the airport parking lot.

It was January deep in a bitter northern winter, about 30 degrees below zero, as I recall. The van's heater wasn't working too well, and when we spoke, our words made little white clouds in the night.

'Have you always lived here?' I asked. 'Were you born here?'

As though I were Aladdin and had suddenly touched the magic spot on a lamp, he turned to me with an air of immense and barely controllable excitement. 'It's there now,' he said, cryptic, intense. 'It's there again, where I was born. I can show you. Would you like to see?'

His eyes glittered in the bitter black air, and so, knowing that whatever this entailed was momentous, I simply said yes. He made a U-turn. Snow barrens stretched as far as the eye could see. Since we'd left the airport, not a single car had passed us either way. We two might have been alone in the universe, under the immense night sky and the stars.

The young Cree Indian (he was about twenty, I think) was lit by some inner radiance. Until this abrupt decision we had talked non-stop, but now silence enfolded us. So great was his excitement, so intense the light within, that an aura shimmered around his body and the van seemed to me full of golden fog. We swung off the road and drove over bumpy packed snow. He was steering either by stars or by instinct. By a grove of scrubby dwarf conifers, he braked sharply and we got out and stood by the shore of a frozen lake, and then he stepped a little way out on the ice and pointed.

'Out there,' he said, transfigured by moon and snow and rapture.

It was the week of his birthday. His mother and grand-mother had been ice fishing on the night of his birth, camped out on the lake, fishing shack tethered to the ice, unstable, when his mother's pains came upon her, sud-denly, early. They were strong women, his mother and grandmother. By the light of tallow candle, on the frozen wafer that ties December to May, inside the smoke-warm shack, his grandmother delivered him into the world. In the morning she pulled the sled containing her daughter and grandson to shore.

The young Cree held his arms out to the moon and the sky and the frozen lake, embracing his history, paying reverence to life itself and to two strong women and to that birthplace which only existed for a few months each year.

He turned to me but could not speak.

I could not speak.

I was overwhelmed by the magnitude of the honour conferred on me.

In that shining moment, stamping my frozen feet on packed snow, the stars so clear and close they could be touched, I swear I smelled the frangipani tree and Breakfast Creek.

The world spins in the margins of space, Australians float in the edges of the world, Queenslanders live in the rind of Australia, I have always drawn breath in the cracks of Queensland.

Queensland itself is fluid in shape and size, it ebbs and flows and refuses to be anchored in space, it billows out like a net that can settle without warning, anywhere, anytime. It is always larger than would appear on the map. There is no escaping it.

Here where I write, where a brilliant cobalt scar of river has just slashed the white surface of March, where the St Lawrence is still mostly skating rink but part flow, I have smelled and touched Queensland. I have woken, disoriented, to see orchids in snowdrifts. Along the bare knotted trunks of maples and hickory trees, epiphyte creepers have run rampant. I have smelled rainforest.

Homeland is where the senses steer by instinct when the reins are let go. It is always accessible in that small space between sleeping and waking.

Down at the bottom of my yard, the St Lawrence sucks

away at the base of our limestone cliffs, it plucks and thaws, plucks and thaws, subtracting from Canada here, depositing American silt there. New York State smudges the horizon. I live at the desiccating edge of things, on the dividing line between two countries, nowhere, everywhere, in the margins.

Wherever I am, I live in Queensland. I know to what brown country and to what wet rainforests my homing thoughts will fly in the moment between living and dying, when *desire shall fail, for man goeth to his long home*, and woman too, there where the evening star goes down, and where the first ones and the latecomers make temporary camp together under the violent stars.

Shining on its short stalk, the Evening Star, always there at the clay pan, at the place of the Dugong ... The Evening Star goes down across the camp, among the white gum trees ... It sinks there into the place of the white gum trees, at Milingimbi.

Amen.

Karima

AAMER HUSSEIN

For Janette Turner Hospital
In friendship
You know the borderlines

Listen brother, she says, you can read Urdu, can't you?
I'd like you to read this for me. This picture here, what
do the words under it say? The man in it, you know, yes,
Naeem, he went from Dhaka to Karachi after the troubles
and he's one of our Biharis, his parents were in a camp and
look at him now, such a big star and he sings so beautifully
too, I've seen him on television and I always listen to his
cassettes. He's coming to Wembley? No, I don't think I
could. No, it's just that he looks like my Shahzad.

(Karima. She used to work in the food shop opposite. I'd go
there late in the evening, tired of thinking or writing, for a
pack of cigarettes. I don't know how it began but one night
we talked and soon she started coming up to get her letters
written. Sometimes to someone in Karachi or Pindi, or
sometimes, rarely, to addresses in Dhaka. Her messages
were always the same. I'm well, working hard, sorry I can't
send more money this time, I can't come home, not this year,
how is Bachu? He must have grown so big by now. She didn't
have an address, so all mail should be sent to her care of us.
And then, at the end, she'd ask for news of Shahzad.)

Shahzad was my son, she says, born when I was still a child.
His father was called Badshah. He was hardly older than

me. Born in the old country though, in Patna, before they came away – his parents and mine – when the country was divided by the strong ones. I was born in Dhaka. I always knew my Badshah, always knew that I'd marry him. His parents had a shop that sold provisions, but he was a mechanic. Already working hard when I married him, looking after his mother and younger brother too. He'd sold his father's business and put the money to good use, to set up on his own. We lived quite well. I didn't have to work, though so many women around me did, and some of our neighbours envied me. In the evenings I'd put on a bright fresh cotton sari and white or red flowers in my hair. Sometimes he'd take me in a rickshaw to the cinema. They'd tease me – unkindly, at times – when my man wasn't around, calling us the royal family because of our good food and our happy faces. In our community no one lived beyond their means but we looked as though we did. And when my son was born I called him Shahzad because I thought a king should have a prince for a son, because I wanted to turn their taunts into blessings, because I wanted him to have a hundred times our luck. His father wanted us to go to Karachi. That's where the real rewards could be had. That was where he should have gone in the first place, he said – that's where they spoke our language, that was the real Pakistan. Those Banglas, he said he couldn't really understand them. We always spoke Urdu at home. He could read and write it, too. But I couldn't really understand him. Perhaps I was too young. And I was born in Dhaka, it was the only place I'd ever known, I could speak Bangla like my own tongue. The people, too, they seemed like my own. But these were matters for men and the old people, who remembered the old country, remembered something better, and told us of what they'd had to sacrifice to bring us to this new land, where we could follow our beliefs in peace, live our lives in peace. But what peace? My boy was two when the troubles came. Perhaps his name had tempted fate. Perhaps I shouldn't have been so happy. Perhaps my husband shouldn't have loved his country so much. Because suddenly East Pakistan wasn't going to be his country any more. It was changing names.

(Karima. One of those ageless women with figure and features carved from ebony. When she loosened her hair it looked like a black storm-wind. She spoke the rapid Bihari Urdu of Dhaka but over the years I knew her it acquired an even more pronounced Bengali intonation and a strong overlay of English words. How old must she be now? Was she thirty-three when she first came to see us, all those years ago, when we helped her with her papers, when her man slapped her, and all those other times when life became too much for her? Well, almost – life will never be too much for Karima. I changed addresses and stopped thinking about her, life doesn't take me her way all that often. Anti-Muslim tracts, the BJP, sectarianism and fundamentalism, desolation over the Gulf War – the computerization of my writing, failure to read Foucault, distaste for Derrida and deconstruction – and yet again my stories hadn't earned me the fare home. No time to spare, to write letters for Karima. Maya would see her at the shelter sometimes, she'd bring her man to the community centre twice a year on Eid, and helped out with the crèche when she wasn't working in their shop till midnight. But then Maya left the shelter for a job in the media and life doesn't take her that way all that often.

Karima. She used to talk so freely she'd shock me sometimes. But there are things she wouldn't talk about. I've seen too much, she'd say, and fall into silence.)

– Brother, don't ask me to tell you about the camp, she says, how can you expect me to remember anything about it?

Crowding, filth, hunger, people complaining. We'd lost everything. Later I went out with the other women to sell things in the city – pencils, feathers, whatever we could lay hands on – while our men found work in factories, did the jobs that men in that rich city would never do. They called us refugees. But how could we be? If the only home we'd ever known had cast us away because we were suddenly foreigners, how come we were foreigners here, too, in Pakistan, the country where we were supposed to belong? Homeless here, homeless there. Sometimes the shit-stink of those camps still fills my nostrils and I think of it as the smell of fear.

Long live Pakistan. He was still shouting those words as he lay dying, my man. Those last terrible days in Dhaka. My boy was two years old. First the Punjabi soldiers had come in from across the sea and begun to pillage around the edges of the city, so people said, and people said that Bengalis and Biharis alike should run for their skins. There were stories of massacres – of students, peasants, passers-by. But Badshah said the soldiers were our friends and they'd come to rescue us from those marauding Banglas. And then even the neighbours began to turn on us. They'd always loved me, I was young and pretty, shared food with them and didn't really mind their teasing. Because I often wore yellow they said I looked like springtime and called me Basanti. But now they'd changed their faces. Dirty Biharis, they said, go home or we'll get you. That day a group of them, so big, all men, turned up. Some of them were the sons of women we knew. Get out, get out, go to your murdering Punjabi masters, they shouted. But we're not harming anyone, this is our home, said my man in Bangla. So say Joy Bangla, Joy Mukti Bahini, one of them said – Victory to Bangladesh and its liberation army. Another one had seen me, cowering in my thin night sari with the screeching boy in my arms, and he came toward me. Badshah went mad. Out, you Bangla traitors, he said in Urdu. He had a broken bottle in his hand. This is Pakistan. Pakistan Zindabad. I'll live and die in Pakistan. Then die, said the one who'd been ready to attack me, and he set my man on fire. I swear he did. The stench of burning flesh still fills my nostrils. I saw my Badshah burn, still screaming, Long Live Pakistan. He told me to run. At least I think it must have been him. Because those bastards, too, they let me go, and one of them said, in Urdu, Take your child and run. And I did. Through the flames of houses dying, past burning bodies, beneath the stars of the sky veiled in the smoke of shame, amid brothers tearing out each other's throats, I ran. To where God took me. He must have been weeping. Or perhaps He had just turned His face away, who can blame Him if this is what His children do?

– What I remember next is being on that boat to Pakistan. With my mother-in-law and my husband's brother. Memories of the camp are blurred, but the city beside it was dry and cold at night, grey instead of green like green, moist Dhaka where the sun warms your skin even in winter. Those feelings, fire and ice, those my bones remember. Of course I never knew then that my destiny lay in cold cities. All I thought of was my grief, survival, and when I began to regain my senses I thought about my child's future. That's why, when Rahim my husband's brother began to look at me with longing in his eyes, I too began to turn toward him. The women around me – so many of them knew more about men than I did, they'd tie their saris tight when they went into the market place, and wink and smile at customers – the women around me told me I could do much worse by myself and Shahzad than a man who was related to my son by blood. He was younger than me, at least three years. I remember his calf-eyes, his scabby knees and his dirty feet when I first came to his mother's house as a bride. Even then he'd bring me gifts of jasmine buds and guavas. Now,

in our new homeland, I saw him for the first time as a man.
We'd seen too much, our eyes had changed. Grown old.
And after all, how old was I, barely twenty-one? My man
dead, my boy barely speaking, with only my untrained
hands to help me live? And young blood has its needs, too,
you know, sister, and Rahim my husband's brother was
handsome. But I never would forget my Badshah.

– So I married again. Of course my mother-in-law wasn't
happy, but at first I thought that my moment of happiness
had brought the sorrow of her son's death back to her. I
thought that having her grandson with her would console
her and once again, in a new city, we'd bring back to her a
family and some fragment of a new life, however fragile.
For we were in Karachi now, a city bigger than I'd ever
imagined, with tall tower blocks and smelly camels and the
salt stale smell of the nearby sea rushing, gushing into our
nostrils. My husband's brother, now my husband, took me
to the sea once, by Clifton, you could ride tin horses on the
pier and men in Punjabi clothes sold salted peanuts in their
shells and blond children pulled at their mothers' skirts. I
was happy for an hour but then I started weeping. I don't
know whether it was because I missed Badshah who used to
take me for walks and on pleasure-trips, or because the big
heavy men around us reminded me of the Punjabi soldiers
I'd seen in Dhaka, or because among all these strange
people I suddenly felt strange, and foreign, and poor. We
were small and thin and dark and the Urdu we spoke was
alien to the people around us, we could scarcely make them
understand us, even though we thought we were speaking
their language and we understood them quite well. Bengali
log, they called us, but we were Bihari and Pakistani, we
thought, even if we'd never seen Bihar and we were new in
Pakistan. And I was pregnant with Rahim's child, too, and
a heavy belly makes me weep. I don't know why, but I knew
that I'd have a boy. When my second son was born his

father called him Habib but in my heart I called him Badshah after his dead uncle who should have been his father, and when his grandmother began to call him Bachu I often wondered whether we shared a secret name for him, knowing that our lost one had sent us a sign.

– Rahim started work as a chauffeur in a big house in Defence and as soon as I could get Bachu away from my breast I began to work in the same house, nannying, ironing, stitching and looking after the mistress's needs. That went on for years. My mother-in-law was cruel to me, but most of all she was cruel to my older boy. She'd go into rages and shout at him, blaming him for all sorts of things. Her worst outbursts were when she'd accuse him of having brought ill-fortune to the family and sucking out his father's life. As if she'd forgotten that he was two when his father died and it was the big men on top who'd united and divided countries and set brothers against each other to tear out each other's throats and their sisters' wombs. Even today our relatives write to us from Bangladesh, begging us to send them money, begging us to send for them, to bring them to Karachi, to Dubai, to London – anywhere. And Lord, your floods and storms, they respect no one, but love us poor best of all.

– New days of misery had come upon us. Rahim's exhaustion, his sense of not living up to his brother's dreams, his disappointment in the new country where we lived beneath a stairway in two small rooms and shared an outside latrine with other servants from the compound, all served to turn him against the child that was not his son, who reminded him, perhaps, of his older brother, who was one more mouth to feed, one more to clothe and send to school. I'd insisted that Shahzad like his father should learn how to read and write, have a profession, at least live up to his father's memory that way, even if he couldn't go beyond what my dead man had done. We'd always been told that this was the land of money and opportunities, but Rahim felt we only had enough for one child, and that child had to be his son. I felt that Bachu was being taken away from me. I worked all day and the child was looked after by his grandmother. Maji, too, like Rahim, seemed to save all her love for Bachu. She wouldn't feed him when he came back from school, encouraging him to go up to the kitchen of the big house instead to beg the cook for scraps. So I became even more protective of Shahzad, keeping everything for him, my money and my love.

– The boil burst open one day when the children in the big house had a party. They sent for Shahzad, and Maji too went up with Bachu, to keep an eye on the children. Rahim was meant to help serve the fried savouries and sticky cakes and pink pastries while I was in the house, looking after the needs of the fancy ladies. I found out later that Saima, the little miss whose birthday it was, had turned on a big tape-recorder and got all her guests dancing to pop music. At some point she'd called to Shahzad and asked him to dance. Bachu came running to me on his fat legs, telling me to come out and see what was happening up there. I went out, into the garden, where the sun was just setting. Surrounded by a circle of clapping, cheering children, Shahzad was wiggling, twisting, his feet rose and fell, the music had him in thrall. Look at your beloved, said his grandmother. Dancing like a whore, like a eunuch. The boy had told me he wanted to be a star, like those men on television in bright jackets or the heroes in the movies with a song and a swinging step for every occasion, but I'd never listened to him, thinking of his words as a child's rambling dreams.

I grabbed him by the ear and pulled him down to our room. Down there I thrashed him while Maji watched exulting, it was the first time I'd ever hit him, but as I did I swear that I felt that the hand that struck was not mine but his uncle's, and as I flagged Maji came up for her turn and I slapped her as well with the back of my hand. When Rahim drove the Sahib home from his club that night he found us all crying and screaming, and without asking what had happened he gave Shahzad another few slaps and Bachu a smack, too, for good measure. The next day, early, Shahzad was gone, and it was weeks before we had news of him. He'd found a job skivvying for some mechanic. He was twelve years old.

(I picked up a book about the failure of Punjab's Green Revolution from a friend's place on Sunday afternoon, and read about the Sikh farmers and how their discontent derived not from religious differences but landlessness and dispossession. Three days later the book's author was on the box, supporting Malaysia's Mahathir in his diatribe against the North's exploitation of the South while screen images flung Filipino forms, scavenging in muck heaps, at our faces. The rule of Pepsi-cola capitalism. The Earth Summit is nigh. Anger's lava boils on both sides. The rich masters of destinies trade insults on behalf of the deprived. The Third World, convenient category, the forfeit. And I was trying to write about homelessness. Doing my research, my intellectual field-work. On public platforms, or private white paper in poetry or prose, we trace our trajectories of exile and expatriation, claim landless negativity as the writer's preserve and sing homelessness as the eternal ineradicable condition of the human soul. Celebrate the gap between our raw material and our present situation. With pride we assume the mantle of the dispossessed. What lies, what postures. So long since I've even thought about it. I wanted to write something about the Sikh farmers, but I'd been away too long. The smell of a subjective landscape gone. Irreducibles reduced to beckoning banalities. No

grants or awards around for homesickness these days. Plan
to save the price of a plane ticket 'home' dissolves in the
foggy business of living. You shouldn't even think of
'home', it's out of intellectual fashion. Illiterate voices fight
the vagaries of a language too remote to contain them.
Polemic is out, the gentle weave of 'fiction' veils the pain
that mustn't be spoken. Too loud, aggressive or sentimental, simply over the top. This ain't no story, brother, you're
overmining the documentary vein, it's journalism, a tract.

I watched the stub-end of a documentary about Green
Revolution Technology in the Punjab, watched a Bihari
farmer, one of the 'Bhaiyyas', economic refugees migrating
to work in the Punjab these days. They don't have their
own land in Bihar though they have the skill to till the soil
for others, and the money they send back helps the people
at home. The 'Bhaiyya's' tones and mangled verbs brought
back the sound of Karima. Who used to bring me her letters
and her questions and her stories. Bear witness to her, I
wrote that night, in foreign words that she wouldn't
understand.)

– It wasn't too bad in those first days in London, brother,
she says. My salary was being paid in rupees back at home,
and a secret part of it went to Shahzad. He'd promised he'd
come home, continue his schooling. It was only for a short
time. The mistress's son had some strange problem, he
couldn't walk or speak properly, and she'd brought him
here for treatment. One or two years, and then I'd go back
home. The work load, if anything, was lighter than in
Karachi. I slept in the children's room and could watch
two, three Hindi videos in one day. The food was good. In
the afternoon I took the children to the park, the boy in his
push-chair, and I found some other women there. Some of
them talked about being like prisoners, how hard their

employers made life for them. One or two of them were
Bangla. There was also the halal butcher down the road, he
was Bangla too, and he told me about the women and men
who would come here on one pretext or another and just
disappear, into an underworld of sweatshops, restaurants,
groceries, earn their living in pounds and send more money
home than they'd ever imagined. A hard life, but worth it in
the end. It didn't impress me much, then, but what I
thought was that somehow I could bring Shahzad here,
even if I had to go back he could stay, someone like the
Bangla butcher could do with an able-bodied lad like him.
He kept on asking me to come and work a few hours in his
shop, he said a clever woman would be a help and I could
have done with the extra foreign cash, but when I tried to
talk to the mistress she wouldn't hear of it and thought I
was being ungrateful.

– When I'd been here six months the mistress said my
visa was up, I had to go home. I said Sister, if my salary is
too much for you to pay you can send me out to work at the
neighbours', you know they could do with an extra hand, or
I could do a few hours at the butcher's, maybe Saturday or
Sunday. But Karima, she says, I'm going back myself, you
know little Baba's so much healthier now, and it's getting
cold, and your husband wants you home, you've got your
ten-year-old son to think of and your mother-in-law's
getting old and very sick. But my other boy, Sister, I said,
you know I've been sending him money to go to school –
She cut in. Karima, she said, there was an accident . . . your
boy . . . a van . . . Rahim . . . When? I said. My feet had
turned to sunken rocks. The sockets of my eyes were on
fire. Oh . . . six weeks, a month, I think? There didn't seem
to be any point . . . Saheb said your people thought it would
be better if I didn't tell you, after all you'd find out soon
enough at home, and I told him to advance Rahim some
money . . . for the . . . you know, the prayers and all . . .

– I kept quiet. What could I say? The stench of burning flesh, the shit-smell of the camps, the faces of marauders and the scared eyes of the ones who ran, flowed before my eyes. They lived in me. I waited a day. Then I asked for fifteen pounds and an afternoon's leave to buy things for my husband's brother – yes, that's what I called him and the mistress didn't even notice – and my little boy. I left all my things in the flat, took the key with me, and I ran. I walked slowly, proudly, but I ran. The open market was Dhaka on fire, and if I didn't move calmly one side or the other would get me. I made my way to the butcher's shop. His eyes had told me the whole story. I knew I'd have to pay in some way the price of my stay, just a hiding place to start with. At first I was terrified that the mistress would set the immigration people on me because I'd unthinkingly walked away with her key, wanting to go there later to get my stuff, but of course I soon gave up that plan, and no one came after me. Later? I still tremble. That's another story.

– I've been with the butcher seven years now. I stay here alone when he goes to Bangladesh. What if someone recognized me and realized I couldn't be his wife? And how would he explain a strange Bihari wife from London, and what is there for me now in Dhaka? And how could I go with a Bangla man to the city that killed Badshah? But here, we're all the same, Bihari or Bangla. He's only hit me once, when he caught me taking more money from the till than he thought I should for Bachu, because I still send money to the people in Karachi, and always add a little for Shahzad because no one ever wrote from there to tell me that he'd gone. But of course I can't let them have my address – after all, who knows? – Rahim may still remember that he has a wife and somehow turn up here to find me. But maybe the money I send has made him forgive me, if there is anything to forgive. In the end, it's between me and my God. Of course I still think of Bachu, but he never really was mine to start with, and perhaps he's best off with his father. Life isn't any easier here for us, people stare and curse at you on the streets and threaten you in your shop late at night. And the hours are so long. This isn't a good home for our young, when you really think about it.

– When the butcher hit me I packed my stuff and walked off to a place that some Bangla women had told me about, run by women for other women. Some of them spoke Urdu. I stayed there a few days, then I called the butcher from a coinbox and told him where to meet me. When I admitted he was coming to get me from the post office down the road all the women said I was crazy to go back with him, but I explained to them that I'd told him, If you ever hit me again I'll cut you to pieces with your own carving knife, and if you don't pay me my proper share of the takings I'll report you for every petty crime under the sun. My words hadn't really been that hard, but I'd said enough to put the fear of God in him, and I think he wanted in his way to keep me happy.

– I hate these winters, especially when the butcher's away. Letters from my people are rare, and sometimes I wonder if the money I send there ever gets to them. I long for news of Bachu. I have a photograph of him which Maji sent in some moment of pity, but my greatest regret is that in my haste I forgot to pick up my photographs of Shahzad. After I lost him I've stopped feeling anything for Pakistan. Some nights I dream of him, talking to me, telling me he didn't really die, that he lives in the television now and sings there. That's why I collect every picture I can of the singer Naeem and paste it in my album. He's slim and strong, his eyes are like rain-clouds, and his skin shines like copper in the sun. I know that's how my boy would have looked if he'd grown to be a man, because that's what his father was like, and Shahzad was just like my Badshah.

Bad News

LYNNE TILLMAN

'The King of Kings is also the Chief of Thieves. To whom do I complain?'

Ten Ten WINS, ten ten on your dial, the news never stops, the news all the time. You give us twenty-two minutes, we'll give you the world: A black woman in Brooklyn has been murdered. Police report the woman was thrown off her roof after she was raped.

The news is broadcast every twenty minutes, the headlines every few minutes. Then there's TV, two hours of news around dinner time, not counting CNN. Bulletins any time. We interrupt this regularly scheduled program, the announcer says, to bring you this bulletin.

The woman in Brooklyn was raped and murdered in her home. Her body was dragged from her apartment and carried to the roof. By a stranger, the police say. The stranger threw her off the roof. The news didn't give her name.

The news is no stranger. It's always there at the same time, Elizabeth thought. She stayed tuned, hooked to the pain and pleasure of small and great events. At the announcement of disaster, Elizabeth sensed danger as if the bad news were inside her, a shrill wake-up call ringing in her body. Alarmed, occasionally Elizabeth was moved to confess. At least she sometimes felt the urge, but then she laughed at herself. She was guilty but there was nothing to confess and, worse, no one to hear her confession. Definitely a problem, she remarked to her boyfriend, Henry, who replied, in his offhand way, Some days you eat the dog, some days the dog eats you.

Henry and Elizabeth likened each other to animals. To him, she was a small, furry creature, a squirrel or weasel, because she was nervous so much of the time. To her, he was a mule or donkey. Henry was determined and stubborn. Elizabeth poured a cup of coffee and added milk to it until the coffee turned the tawny color she liked.

Murder is ordinary. There are usually three or four a day. I don't want to, but I can see the woman. I can hear her scream. Get out, get out, what do you want, leave me alone, leave me alone, you're hurting me. I can see her body dragged up flights of dirty stairs and carried onto the roof, and I can see her thrown over as if she weren't a human being, just garbage.

At night Elizabeth hailed taxis. It was worth it, she reminded herself each time she paid a cabdriver, it was her life she was saving, not money. Walking on the street Elizabeth masked her fear under a veil of poise and cool. She had read everything she could about serial murderers. Elizabeth knew that Ted Bundy had chosen his victims wisely – they were all troubled women caught by him at a bad time in their lives. Bundy had spotted something in their eyes and had seduced the women easily. Elizabeth tucked her fear inside her body.

Ten Ten WINS: We'll quickly update you on the top stories. Ten Ten WINS every time. All news all the time, stay tuned: It's cloudy in New York, wind from the south at ten miles an hour.

Elizabeth reassured herself with the fact that, apart from serial murders, most women who were murdered were murdered by men they knew or lived with. Elizabeth lived alone, but Henry often slept at her place. He liked her apartment, it was cozy. Elizabeth was sensible about her fear some of the time, and the statistics, the odds, were reassuring. They were on her side.

Elizabeth shook her head up and down and from side to side. Dreamily, she concocted stories she could use, just in case. She would be prepared if she had to plead for her life to a guy high on crack who held a knife to her throat, who would end her life for twenty dollars.

I'm John Gotti's daughter and if you do this to me, if you touch me, just touch me, you'll have to answer to the Mafia. They'll get you if you hurt me. Don't do it. Don't you do it. Don't even think about it. I've got AIDS, rape me, murder me, and you'll die too.

Shame and revulsion crawled over, in and through Elizabeth, an internal rebuke to the self she shared with no one. She disgusted herself – using disease like that, as a threat, a weapon. She wouldn't, ever. But even if she gave the guy money, he might murder her.

I could scream. I could scratch his eyes out. I could kick him in the balls. I could fight him with all my strength. I'd scream for help. I'd scream bloody murder. But what if no sound came out of me? In nightmares I can't move, I can't run away. I'm glued to the spot where I'm in danger. Maybe I won't be able to move. Then they'd say, she died without a struggle. I'd be pathetic.

Elizabeth knew a woman who carried a small hatchet in her handbag. She envisioned her friend taking the hatchet from her bag. In the scene the would-be murderer, rapist, or mugger was surprised, bemused or terrified. Then he ran away. Her friend was safe. But Elizabeth didn't think the woman would be able to reach into her bag and grab the hatchet, to strike a deadly blow with deadly force. She wondered if she herself would be able to cross the narrow line that separated her life and body from another's.

Maybe my friend would hit him in the head with the sharp edge of the ax. She'd split his head in half. Blood would gush from his head. There would be blood everywhere, all that blood from one body. My friend wouldn't be able to do it. She'd hit him with the blunt side of the ax. I don't know if I'd be able to do it. I don't know if I could count on myself.

Ten Ten WINS, news all the time: On the question of the safety of nuclear reactors a scientist explains that safety means an acceptable level of risk. There is some risk in everything.

Elizabeth pictured the woman in her apartment in Brooklyn. Just over the bridge. Not very far away. The woman was fighting for her life. Elizabeth pushed the ugly scene from her mind and looked out the window at some sparrows on a roof. A few birds were also on the bare branches of the tree in the garden. They had not flown south, because people had begun feeding them during the winter. They were plump and content. As she gazed at them, Elizabeth smoothed her hair. It was an unconscious gesture. Her fingers found a few thick, wiry hairs which she touched with pleasure.

On CNN, on television, there were images of people dead and dying, wounded and bleeding. Though broadcast in color, there was something about war that was always in black and white, something direct and obvious. Incontrovertible. In its horrifying way war was, to Elizabeth, comforting. She knew what it was and so did everyone else. War is everyone's perfect stranger, the strangest and most normal of events. Everyone knows who's suffering and which people need help, and there's no question about that. It's a relief to know. Elizabeth imagined the woman in Brooklyn. She was cowering in her kitchen.

Ten Ten WINS, news all the time, Ten Ten WINS takes you there: Five people were found shot to death, execution-style in Queens. The police report it was drug-related. The news watch never stops. You give us twenty-two minutes, we'll give you the world. WINS News Time 10:22.

Elizabeth let her breath out slowly. When she visualized her feeling in words – something like 'I breathed a sigh of relief' – she laughed at herself again. Drug-related murders didn't count. Everyone knew if you weren't in the business, no one messed with you. You were safe. Still, life was a series of violations and people were shot and knifed daily. Sometimes by mistake.

I could be in the way. I could be in the wrong place at the wrong time. But it's really surprising that more of us aren't knifed every day. People look so crazy. I can see it in their eyes, any minute they might leap out of their skins and into someone else's or onto someone else. Just to get themselves straight, just to get rid of something, just to lose themselves, just not to be in themselves for a second. Everyone says how violent the city is, but actually, considering how things are, it's not so bad, not that dangerous. It could be much worse. I'm safe enough.

Elizabeth remembered Ricky. He lived downstairs before his grandmother sent him away. He was running toward the corner to buy dope. There's a bust, Elizabeth told him. She was as cool as ever. Better not go that way now. She described the cops who were holding four young guys up against the wall. She had watched along with several other whites, some Latinos and blacks. Everyone was fascinated, staring, waiting, for something. Maybe the cops would go berserk, turn violent. Elizabeth described to Ricky how the four guys were searched, against the wall, their legs and arms spread apart. Ricky listened and turned around. They walked home together. He told her she had it easy. From his point of view she had it made.

If I screamed, if Ricky were around, he would come to

my aid. I know he would, he likes to fight. And deep down, inside him, he's OK. But it doesn't matter. It doesn't matter what anyone feels inside. If someone needed money desperately, or if some guy hated his mother or hated everyone and everything, if someone was totally deranged, and I was there, at the wrong time, it wouldn't matter. That's it. It would be all over.

Ten Ten WINS, all the time, every time: you can count on us twenty-four hours a day. Fifty-three degrees. We're heading down to forty-seven. Ten Ten WINS: The U.S. government is sending the Haitian refugees back to Haiti. It has determined that they are not political refugees. Their problem is economic, the government says, not political. Stay with Ten Ten WINS for all the news all the time.

I'm living in something I don't understand. It's crazy. Everyone thinks so. I'm morbid. I think about dying too much. Even Alice thinks I'm being irrational. I should keep it to myself. I look perfectly normal. I have a job. I have a roof over my head. I have nothing to complain about. It's life, Henry says, get used to living it.

Elizabeth and Henry were having breakfast. The wallpaper, like inkblots, loomed crazily around the kitchen table. Henry watched as Elizabeth selected four slightly tan, nearly lavender eggs from the refrigerator shelf. Then Henry sliced the bread. Later Elizabeth studied him as he looked out the window. She could hear him breathe. His fragility was what she loved best about him. She thought of the word tender and imagined how it would appear in neon. She told Henry who said he'd do that for her, for her next birthday. He said he'd bend that neon to his will. He always made her laugh.

Ten Ten WINS, NEWS ALL THE TIME, YOU GIVE US TWENTY-TWO MINUTES WE'LL GIVE YOU THE WORLD.

The news didn't mention the woman in Brooklyn anymore. That was old news, and other murders took its place. Henry repeated a joke he'd heard the night before. Two bags of vomit were walking along the street. One became sentimental and cried. The other asked, Why are you crying? The first said, I was brought up around here.

After Henry left, Elizabeth lingered in the kitchen and read the small, unimportant items at the bottom of the newspaper's long pages.

I'm one of the little people, a little woman. An ordinary person. One of the common people. Our lives are just territory for bombs and soldiers to land on. In war, one person's life in the middle of all the horror and chaos is nothing. In war civilians might be wounded, or killed by rampaging troops, by incensed soldiers trained to hit hard, to take no prisoners. Getting murdered is nothing. It happens all the time. There doesn't have to be a war. Our bodies get landed on every day. Our insides are carved up and churned over and spit out into nothing, they become nothing. Anyone can be the enemy. Everyone is strange.

Just by looking at her neighbors, Elizabeth hoped to ascertain who was reliable, who could be counted on late at night if someone lurked in the doorway. She couldn't decide whether it was good or bad that three new bodegas had opened up on her block and were selling drugs. Now people hung around all the time, but she didn't know if any of the guys running the drug stores would go out of his way to help her. Still, murder was bad for business. It wasn't street smart. It brought the cops and unwanted attention, so the dealers, she thought, might try to stop it from happening.

I could be dragged off the street by a guy in a car who had a gun. It could happen in an instant and not draw any attention. No one might even see it. The next day it would be a small item in the newspaper. Woman Raped and Murdered. Maybe because I'm white, it would be given more space. Depends on the city desk, if it's a slow news day or not. People who didn't know me would be happy not to be me. Everyone would be happy not to be a murder victim. People could say, even friends, she shouldn't have lived in that neighborhood, she should have known it was dangerous. It was stupid, they'd say, her death was avoidable.

Elizabeth understood she couldn't be protected, not from the unknown or from random violence. Much as he loved her, Henry couldn't be there all the time, and much as she loved Henry, she couldn't save him. Everyone, she thought, was hapless. Henry teased her about being a character trapped in an episode from *The Twilight Zone*. She was waiting to hear her own death reported on Ten Ten WINS. It was a running joke, part of their intimacy.

Ten Ten WINS, all the news all the time: The Pentagon has released figures which show that during the Gulf War, half of our soldiers were killed by friendly fire. Stay with Ten Ten WINS.

Friendly fire was a funny term. Grimly ironic, Elizabeth said to Henry, like murder between friends. Henry claimed that Elizabeth's fear was an escape from reality. She wondered what reality was and who decided. But she kept that to herself. Elizabeth hated to think that her sympathies, and her fears, if held up to the harsh light of reality, would be found wanting and incomprehensible. She herself might be found wanting, insufficient. She hated that.

Like Having God Pay You a Visit

JOSEF SKVORECKY

One day Mother opened a letter just delivered by the mailman and said: 'We have a grandfather!' I was shocked because Mom always insisted that in my case there is no grandad. She herself came into this world without the help of a male parent, which explained why Grandma passed on during the delivery. Mom, of course, takes me for an underage idiot, which I am not. I've known for a long time, that some sort of a grandfather does exist somewhere, an illegitimate one, naturally, who took off, most likely to avoid obligations.

The letter confirmed that, but it explained that the turmoil of war separated Grandad from Grandma and in the ensuing chaos he could never find her. On the basis of Mom's birthdate I determined by reading a history text book that Grandad most likely fought in Korea.

However, when Grandad arrived in Canada where Mom invited him immediately, despite Dad's objections of a financial nature, he explained the matter quite differently than in the original written draft. According to the new oral account Grandad was too busy as a builder of socialism, and he entrusted Mother in her infantility to a socialist institution, and then forgot about her existence in the tumult of fierce creation, being, as he was, responsible for much more important matters of public welfare. I didn't know what he meant by the word 'builder', but Grandad made it clear to me, that it is someone who covers himself in glory. To my question about the meaning of the word 'socialism' he answered that it is highest justice. Apparently it is the same that we in our language in Canada call God, or Jehovah, as for instance when Mom threatens Dad that she will leave him and go with Dr Jerry Prochaska and 'not even Jehovah himself will help you', referring thereby to Father's religion, while she herself plays the guitar at the Jesuit Fathers' services.

I liked Grandad from the first moment. He explained that he suddenly remembered Mother when, as a People's Lay Judge, he sentenced both my parents to the forfeiture of all property and two years of corrective detention for leaving the republic illegally. Over there something like that is a crime, because their republic is scientifically rearranged. Which Canada isn't. I figured out that unlike Canada which is a monarchy, the People's Republic is a theocracy, from which it then naturally follows that over there everything can be a crime. Because as Father O'Reilly teaches us at Sunday School, God is omnipotent, the same as Jehovah, and what he orders must happen. When Grandad remembered his forgotten daughter, he suddenly longed for her with paternal feelings so intense that he made up his mind to visit her in Canada at all costs. These were covered by Dad, who paid for the air fare on Air Canada.

Arriving from the airport, Grandad sat down in the living room, looked around, and said: 'Terrible furniture! What 'you call this junk anyway, for chrissake? A couch?'

'Brazilian real leather,' Mom answered proudly, because the couch cost $850.

'And that cupboard?'

'Danish teak,' said Dad the same way, i.e. proudly, because for the cupboard, the record cabinet, and the liquor cabinet he paid a total of $1,247.26, and he had to take a loan from the Royal Bank.

'And this table, or whatever it is?' Grandad looked into the kitchen which together with the living room forms one space.

'American Colonial Style,' said Mom. 'That's original, we bought it at an antique store.'

Then Grandad looked at the bedroom where everything is made of African mahogany, and asked: 'So how much did it set you back, all told?' And when Dad with obvious pride said: 'A little over $8,000,' Grandad chuckled and said: 'How can you live in all this junk and not go out of your mind? Such cosmopolitan mishmash! Where are your folk roots?! You are my daughter – where's your national pride?! No more! That's it! Enough is enough! Vlastimila, I was originally a carpenter – I am going to build you new furniture. Real folk furniture! Anyway, what would I do here, in this capitalistic system of yours? I don't like sightseeing! And I don't want any backtalk!'

Dad and Mom started to object, saying that Grandad was their guest and that he should take it easy, that they couldn't take advantage of his kindness. But he stopped them and said: 'And it'll cost you all of $4,148, fair and square.' I was fascinated by the amazing accuracy with which Grandad estimated the price of the job, which he hadn't even started, not knowing the cost of materials on the Canadian market, but it certainly took Mom's and Dad's breath away. After a while they started to protest again, they can't have Grandad doing such hard work, but Grandad wouldn't hear of it, insisting on making folk furniture, and in the end he carried out his intentions.

I liked how Grandad talked, but he on the vice versa didn't. 'W'at kind a' gobbledygook is that: *Grandad*?' he'd say, all upset. 'And I ain't grabbing no subway on my way home. I ain't no thief! Speak Czech to me, your mother tongue, and remember: to me you ain't no Derek, no way. Your proper Czech name is Dmytrij!'

I always thought that Dmytrij was Russian, but then I said to myself that Grandad *must* know what he's talking about and that I'd learn to speak Czech properly from him, which I soon did. Mom couldn't keep up with me because her Czech is already corrupted beyond repair. For instance one day when Grandad was in the living room building some of the new furniture, Mom asked me in the backyard by the pool what Grandad was doing. I said: 'He's covering himself in glory,' and Mother said:

'Really? What you are trying to say is: he's guzzling beer. Right?'

That wasn't what I was trying to say, but it too was true.

With Grandad's arrival our lives changed very radically. For instance: before, Mom and I used to eat a hamburger or a sandwich for lunch, and for dinner chicken or beef with vegetables, because Mom and Dad are afraid of being overweight. As soon as I caught sight of Grandad I knew that he wasn't. And I was right. 'You're skinny as a rake, Vlastimila,' he said right away, 'and that husband of yours likewise. Skin and bones. You'll come down with TB. There's gonna be some proper eating 'round here!' he decided. And there was. From that day on, so that Grandad shouldn't worry about all of us getting TB, Vlastimila (which is Czech for Vicky, which is my Mom's real name) prepared hot food three times a day, and cold food twice, which Grandad referred to in Czech as jauzepauze. Dad said it was a German word, but Grandad thought he was getting too smart for his own good. First day we had hamburgers for lunch which Mom prepared from ground beef, Grandad ate ten of them, which was all she made. Then he said he never wanted to eat such crapola again.

Mom gave me two dollars to fetch two more crapolas from
McDonald's for the two of us, me and herself. The same
thing happened at dinner when Grandad ate both of the
Swiss Chalet chickens, bones and all, and then said that
next time he wasn't interested in eating mosquitoes. Again
I went secretly to McDonald's for crapolas, and wondered
that in Czechoslovakia people probably didn't know about
chickens since Grandad thought they were bugs. And I was
fascinated by the size of their mosquitoes. Later on, however, having listened to Grandad night after night, I
understood: in Czechoslovakia everything is better and
bigger, and there is more of it than in Canada. From that
day onwards Mom never served Grandad crapolas or
mosquitoes, but only roast pork, dumplings, and sauer-
kraut, or sauerbraten with dumplings.

While working, Grandad was in the habit of drinking
beer directly from the bottle at a speed which I calculated
on my pocket calculator: 4.36 bottles per hour. That is, he
worked a total of eleven hours a day (6–12 a.m. and 1–7
p.m.) and used one carton (twenty-four bottles) in the
morning and one in the afternoon. After dinner he always
drank half a bottle of plum brandy made by Jelinek, who
now owns his own liquor factory in Mississauga, Ontario.
He left his country and ended up in Canada on the garbage
dump of history, Grandad said.

Another time, under the influence of capitalist plum
brandy, Grandad told us about the greatest moments of his
life, the largest of which was the moment in 1951 when he
saw with his own eyes in the Kremlin C'mradestalin. I
didn't know who C'mradestalin was as my parents never
told me, but Grandad explained it to me: 'C'mradestalin
knew and anticipated everything,' he said. 'If we'd
followed C'mradestalin, Dubček never would have
happened!'

I deduced that C'mradestalin who knows everything,

even ahead of time, and can make time stop, is just another term for God or Jehovah, or socialism, which all in all is the same thing.

But my good old Dad said:

'Grandad, you know what went on. In 1951 when you were in Russia, didn't anything strike you as really strange?'

By then Grandad had already given up on improving my good old Dad's Czech, and he just said:

'First of: those were all lies made up by that revisionist Khrushchev. And second of: the responsibility for them massacres cannot be pinned on C'mradestalin. And third of: it says something about my class instinct, that when I came back from Moscow to Prague, I said in a meeting: C'mrades, I said, they're all beautiful c'mrades, admirable, especially C'mradestalin himself, then also Molotov, Coctail, Lysenko, Wakeupoff – all of them, except that Beria. I don't know about that one. He's a shrivelled-up little kike –' and Grandad rolled his eyes at Father and said: 'And as it turns out I was right. It was that kike Beria who was responsible for the violations of socialist justice and other deviations. C'mradestalin knew about none of it. And it's clear-as-day that that kike Beria was just the extended arm of international Jewdom –'

'Dad,' Dad interrupted him. 'I am Jewish!'

'Bullshit!' Grandad halted.

'I am,' said Dad, his face red. 'You want to see?' and he reached down to unzip his fly.

'Oto!' said Mom threateningly. 'Control yourself. And you Dad –'

'Whoa! Hold your horses!' said Grandad quickly. ''course, I got nothing against Jews as such. I got Jews among some of my best friends. What I wanted to say was Zionist. Berla was an extended arm of international Zionism!'

'I am also a Zionist!' Dad said, turning even redder. 'You want to see?'

'Oto!' shouted Mom, although this time Father didn't put his hand on his zipper, reaching into his breast pocket instead.

'What are you blabbering?' Grandad called out angrily. 'Stop shitting me or I'll deck you!'

Dad pulled a card out of his pocket. It looked just like a credit card and he showed it to Grandad.

'Card-carrying Zionist,' he said. 'I became a member of this organization here in Canada, Dad, because your Party raised my consciousness as a Jew.'

'STOP SHITTING ME!' roared Grandad. 'Y'think I was born T'DAY? I've had my indoctrination! IN-DOC-TRI-NATION!! You won't shit ME with any Zionist bullshit!'

Grandad seemed very upset and Dad became hesitant.

'Here, read it for yourself,' he said and poked his card at Grandad.

'DON'T INSULT MY INTELLIGENCE!' roared Grandad. 'What d'you think I am? A stupid UNAFFI-LIATED IDIOT? You think that I think that junk like THAT,' and he swept the card out of Father's hand onto the floor, 'something like THAT is a problem to come by in your CAPITALISTIC SYSTEM? At Niagara didn't you yourself have real American dollar bills made up with my own picture instead of Lincoln, so that the c'mrades back home would shit 'emselves? Didn't you have a whole newspaper printed up with an article about me, how I screwed an underaged girl in a helicopter which can be rented for flying over the falls, so that I could pull one over the c'mrades back at the organization? And you think you can shit ME with that garbage? What's a stupid member-ship card compared to GAGS LIKE THAT!?'

'But Dad –' tried my good old Dad.

'Now look 'ere!' roared Grandad and grabbed Dad by the lapels. 'You can't pull that on me! I KNOW EVERY-THING ABOUT ZIONISM!'

'Movement –' stammered Dad.

'It's a TACTICAL EVASION which the Party uses for CERTAIN PURPOSES, necessary in the CLASS STRUGGLE!' roared Grandad at the top of his voice. 'You're gonna try and tell me that something like that really exists! ME? Every morning I read the Party paper. The *Rude Pravo!* That's almost like the *PRAVDA!* Every day, you pansy, every day our Party organ writes about Zionism. AND THE WHOLE OF YOUR ROTTEN BOURGEOIS WORLD HAS BOUGHT IT. LOCK, STOCK, AND BARREL! You gonna feed me that bull-shit! I've got the Order of Merit and the Memorial Medal for –' and at that point Grandad suddenly stopped. 'Damn it – for what? Shit, it just slipped my mind. But me, an honorary member of the Society for Anmity. Me?! ME!!'

Then Grandad left the dining room and went to his room, where we heard him roaring for a very long time. Although I didn't really understand what was being discussed, I liked Grandad. He definitely had charisma.

The furniture that Grandad eventually produced was beautiful and lots of fun. It had different shapes, not like our old cosmopolitan junk, and it had colourfully designed art all over it, like you find on playing cards, hearts and green leaves, etcetera, which Grandad calls character. Some of the pieces had angles, others had curves. It was artistic furniture, like I saw when Mother, who is studying for a Canadian M.A. in cinematographic sciences with Professor Tabborski, took me to see *The Cabinet of Doctor Caligari.* 'Well, you know, Vlasta,' Grandad said, 'I didn't do no cabinet-making for thirty years. I was more in politics, so there might a tiny fault here and there. But you can see the craft – it's got that!' I forgot to ask Grandad what he meant by the word 'craft', but I deduced it from the way the furniture worked during the special dinner that my parents gave on Grandad's insistence, to show off their new furniture.

It played tricks on everyone. It started first off when Dr Cvalavec sat in a new chair. A shiny spring popped up vibrating between his legs through the upholstery, hit his glasses, and threw them right across the room, where they landed on the nose of Miss Milly Franek, who was just coming in through the door. So you see, the furniture was full of surprises and from the very beginning everyone had lots of fun with it.

I'll admit that the fun the furniture was having was sometimes a little bit rough. For instance when Father Sanda stood his cup of coffee on the coffee table, and the cup sort of melted into the table up to its rim, and when it cooled down it stayed that way, and Father Sanda had to sip his coffee through a straw, hunched over the table. The cup is still there; they couldn't get it to come out. I don't think anyone has such a great coffee table.

Or listen to this one! like when Mrs Knapp's wrap-around skirt got caught in the seat of the folk-art chair, because the slats spread apart when you sat down, and came back together when you stood up, so that the wrap-around skirt got caught between the slats and unwrapped, and Mrs Knapp stood there suddenly in her pantyhose, which no one minded, not even Mrs Knapp, I figure, because she's stacked.

Finally, third off, I myself, when Mom put me in a high chair, suddenly felt the seat going down under me, and there were four rods towering over me. Grandad cleverly drilled the holes for the rods somewhat larger, so that when I sat in it, I slowly pushed the seat downwards. But all they had to do was turn the chair over and sit me on the opposite end. Immediately the seat started to go down again, but they put the Oxford Dictionary under it, and that fixed it.

Soon after that we took Grandad to the Toronto airport, where he took an Air Canada direct flight to Prague, the price of the return ticket having been prepaid by my Dad.

Grandad was carrying $4,148.00 in cash, which was the exact estimate of the price of the furniture. Father got the money partly through the sale of our old furniture and partly by a loan from the Royal Bank.

We all said goodbye with tears in our eyes.

'Come again, Dad,' said Mom very quietly. She didn't seem sure of herself. But Dad, on the other hand, said very resolutely: 'That's for sure!'

'Grandad!' I shouted and kissed him. 'Come back soon, come and visit us at the garbage dump of history!'

The plane took off and soon disappeared in the clouds.

A week later a letter from Grandad arrived in which he spoke very critically about capitalism. In the six months that he stayed with us inflation affected the value of the Canadian dollar so much that for his $4,148.00 he could now get at the foreign exchange store Tuzex only $3,871.25. 'Fine gratitude I've lived to see,' wrote Grandad, 'for my effort to create a pleasant folk-inspired living space. Knowing that you live in difficult conditions of exploitation, I didn't want to burden you financially, I just wanted to make enough money to buy the cheapest car, the two-door Fiat 127. But now, due to the drop in the capitalistic rate of exchange, all I can afford to buy is the Lada 2106 for $3,773! All of the c'mrades in our group have *at least* the Fiat 127! Our C'mrade Chairman, whose son –

having acknowledged his error and normalized his relationship with his old homeland – works for Exxon in Venezuela, actually drives a Renault 20TL for $9,091! And I'm supposed to go around in a Lada 2106? I'll be the laughing stock! And they'll all feel sorry for me, for having such ungrateful children abroad!'

'What's Tuzex?' I asked Mom.

'Buzz off, Derek,' said Mom in English and added in her corrupted Czech: 'It's what's referred to in the Bible as "a mess of pottage".'

'What's pottage?' I asked, but all Mom answered was: 'Oh fuck off, toddler!' and I didn't have the heart to irritate her any further. She was probably missing Grandad.

That is why I don't know the meaning of Tuzex, or pottage. But I do admire Grandad. He most definitely did have charisma.

(Translated by Michal Schonberg. *From a tape recording by Derek MacHane, Grade Two student at the Dwight O'Mackey Elementary School in Etobicoke, Ontario.*)

Brief Encounters

ROBERTA ALLEN

This is not the sort of bar where one expects to find the Commercial Counsellor of the Bulgarian Embassy. With his handlebar mustache, he looks as though he stepped out of the nineteenth century.

'I want to order something very American. What would you suggest?' he says, with a strong accent.

'How about Jack Daniels?' I reply.

'What's that?'

'Bourbon.'

'All right,' he says, smiling.

'How would you like it?' I ask.

'Oh, any way the Americans drink it,' he says.

'Well, do you want ice, soda, or water?'

'Anything you want to give me will be fine,' he says.

Someone has played a song by Prince on the juke box. The Bulgarian nods his head in time to the beat. 'This is a place to see a slice of New York life,' he says, glancing down the bar at the construction crew – my regular customers – who are arguing over a Mets game.

'How long have you been here?' I ask.

'Two years,' he says, 'but soon I will go back to Bulgaria for a new assignment. I lived in Argentina before I came here. I've lived in many countries.'

'What does a Commercial Counsellor do?' I ask.

'I sell Bulgarian products to foreign companies. Every-one thinks Bulgaria is a backward nation – and in many ways it is: we are still largely agricultural, but we make very good tractors, for example, that we sell very cheap.'

'It must be hard moving from place to place,' I say.

'No, I enjoy living in different countries. But it's harder for my wife. She doesn't like to move around so much especially now that we have a little daughter. Are you French?'

'No.'

'You look French. I could swear you are French.'

'I'm not.'

Narrowing his eyes as if to see me better, he says, 'You don't seem quite at ease.'

'Well, I'm new at this,' I reply.

'It shows,' he says, smiling, 'but I think you're charming.'

'Thank you.'

The word 'charming' sounds strange here.

The Bulgarian keeps glancing at a picture of the Beatles, screen printed on a mirror hanging over the bar.

'I like that picture. I really like that picture! Could I buy it?' he asks.

'I'm not the owner. You'd have to ask him,' I say.

Mr M, my boss, has something for every taste in this bar.

'I really want that picture. That is America to me! That would be the perfect memento to bring back to Bulgaria!'

'Well, he usually calls late in the afternoon. I can ask him for you.'

I wonder if he knows that the Beatles are English.

A young Scottish waiter from a nearby restaurant sits down beside him.

'How are you today?' I ask.

'Could be better,' he says. 'Last night I lost a big tip. This group of women came in and drank away their money before they ordered dinner. They didn't know the restaurant doesn't take credit cards.'

The Bulgarian looks at him. I don't think he's met many off-duty waiters in New York.

'The restaurant is nearby?' he asks, in a friendly way.

'Just two blocks over on Second.' He turns to me, 'I'll have Jack on the rocks.'

'Did you order Jack Daniels?' asks the Bulgarian.

The waiter nods.

'That's what I'm drinking too. Very American, hmmm?'

'I guess so,' the waiter says.

'Where do you come from?' asks the Bulgarian.

'Scotland, but I worked my way through France and Germany before I came here.'

'Oh,' says the Bulgarian. 'So you know something of Europe. Let me buy your drink.'

'Cheers!' says the waiter, lifting his glass.

A heavy red-haired woman sits down a few seats away.

'Oh, I need something strong,' she says, with an accent. 'I'll have a scotch and soda.' She looks around the bar. 'I've passed this place a thousand times, but I've never been inside. It doesn't look so bad,' she says, surprised. 'I rarely drink in the afternoon, but I'm so upset today! Do you have children?'

'No.'

'Well, I wish I never had! The way my daughter treated me this afternoon makes me sorry I ever gave birth! Imagine having a daughter who walks several paces behind you on the street because she's ashamed that you're her mother! She's too good for me now – a stock-broker!

'We argued on the street over where to have lunch. We couldn't go where anyone might know her – she didn't say that but that's what she meant so I walked off without saying a word and left her standing on Fifth Avenue. But I feel terrible! What should I do?'

'Talk to her,' I say.

'She'll deny everything – tell me it's all in my head, but I'm no fool.'

'I think you should try,' I say. 'I'm sure she's upset too.'

She sighs, 'You're probably right.'

I serve more beer to the construction crew who are laughing like schoolgirls at the other end of the bar, and bring another round to the Bulgarian and the waiter who seem to have a lot to say to one another.

'I could still swear you are French,' the Bulgarian says to me.

'I'm no more French than I was half an hour ago,' I reply.

The Bulgarian laughs. I think the Jack Daniels is going to his head. 'Let me have a beer too,' he says, glancing at the construction crew, still in high spirits. Two of them are having a mock fight while the others cheer them on.

The red-haired woman looks over at the Bulgarian. 'Do you have children?' she asks.

'Yes, I have a daughter, three years old,' he says.

'Mine is twenty-eight, a stockbroker. She was born here, but I'm from Egypt, and so was her father. I guess that's not the right background for a stockbroker. She should have socialite parents on Park Avenue I suppose. I bet she doesn't tell her friends that her mother's a registered nurse from Egypt.'

The Bulgarian looks impatient. 'Egypt! Bulgaria! Scotland!' he says, waving his hands in the air. 'What difference does it make? Everyone here comes from some place else. That's what makes this city so interesting,' he says, smiling at the woman.

She looks sorry that she spoke.

The Bulgarian is drinking faster and faster. I pour less Jack in his drinks, but it doesn't seem to help.

'This is a pleasant place to spend the afternoon,' he says to me, cheerfully, but his words are slurred. This is one sign of drunkenness I didn't have to learn in bartending school.

The woman drinks two more rounds, and leaves a large tip on the bar. 'I feel better,' she says to me, rising from her seat. 'I'm going to call my daughter when I go home, and get everything off my chest. I was afraid to tell her how I feel, but now I have more courage. I'll let you know how it went,' she says, smiling.

When the waiter gets up to leave, the Bulgarian looks at his watch, surprised. 'I never imagined it was this late!'

He takes a last look at the picture of the Beatles as he rises, gripping the bar for support. 'I still want that picture,' he says. 'I'll have to come back soon.'

I watch him stagger toward the door.

'Don't worry. I won't let anyone else buy it,' I say though I'm sure he won't be back. I wonder whether I'll see the woman from Egypt again, but my thoughts are interrupted by the sudden laughter of the construction crew who are ready for another round of beers.

Nach Unten

JANICE KULYK KEEFER

I am on the Bloor Street bus with Annie – she is taking me
home with her to the bungalow she and her husband
bought after they sold the huge brick house downtown. We
have long since exhausted her store of questions about the
health of my parents and my sister and my brother, and so
we ride side by side in silence. This is not just a matter of
my being young enough to be Annie's granddaughter, and
yet knowing no more about her than that I've always known
her. Perhaps the truest reason for our silence is that the only
language we have between us is still foreign ground to
Annie, though she's lived in Canada for over half her life.
Sometimes I hear English people saying things like, 'Fifty
years since they got off the boat and they still can't speak a
proper sentence – can't pronounce even the simplest
words.' English people, you understand, are not necessarily from Britain: they are simply those who are born with
the language like a silver spoon inside their mouths, who
say Winnipeg instead of Veenipeg, Thunder and not
Toonder Bay. They are the ones who have never been
anywhere but home; who are disobliged when people who
have lost everything but their lives go on carrying the one
thing that will never abandon them.

The silence between Annie and myself is camouflaged by
the fact that so many other people are talking. Across from
us is an old, old woman with a face that could have been
made out of flour, water and a rake. What is left of her hair

has been dyed the colour of the liver spots on her hands. The woman is talking in a high, precise voice to a man with a cast on his leg. They are speaking of their parents, of aunts and uncles a long time dead. 'Epsom salts,' she is saying. 'Every morning they drank a mixture of Epsom salts and lemon juice, and they never knew a day's sickness. No arthritis, and not a wrinkle on their faces.'

I smile at Annie but there's no response – she is staring at a child sitting further down the aisle. The girl is no older than five or six – her red socks and bright black shoes stick out over the edge of the seat, where an adult's knees would be. In her long, straight hair are barrettes shaped like flowers; her hair has the sheen of snow, and perhaps it's this that makes her eyes so blue, like blocks of azure or cerulean in a brand new paint box. Annie is smiling at the child, who has been warned, no doubt, never to speak to strangers, never to let them speak to her, even this silent kind of speech in which all the bones of Annie's face seem to lift and tilt. For a moment it's as if everything this woman has been burdened with – the years and years of labour in a foreign land and foreign tongue – slides off the shelf of her bones and is gone, leaving her as light as something still unborn.

The child folds her hands and begins to sing, first under her breath, then loud enough that I catch a few words: *nach unten geh'n, nach unten, nach unten*. It is a refrain of some kind, perhaps to a nursery rhyme or folk song. The child's mother looks at us uncertainly – this is not, she feels, correct behaviour for the bus. She whispers something to the child, who stops singing and stares into the windows of her bright, black shoes. Annie tugs my sleeve: this is our stop. She doesn't look after the bus as it pulls away, but points to her house, three doors down. It seems to be a point of pride with her that the stop is so close to her house, as though the Toronto Transit Commission had arranged this for her private convenience. Perhaps she feels this makes up for the noise and rush of the street; for the small brick box in which she has to spend her days.

It looks, in fact, no bigger than a gingerbread house. As we walk inside I keep thinking of the other house, the one Mike and Annie bought for a song when people like my parents were moving from old, dark, three-story houses downtown into suburban split-levels with picture windows and prodigious lawns. Annie always kept as lush a garden as she could: summer after summer her narrow city yard would bear bushels of rhubarb and runner beans, onion and garlic, strawberries and cherries. '*Berih*;' she'd say to my mother: '*Yeest*. There's just the two of us – you have a family to feed.' And so we'd take and eat the food from Annie's garden, until even strawberries lost their savour, and there was no room on our cellar shelves for all her jars of pickles and preserves.

Mike is watching television; Annie simply turns down the volume, letting the colours blare instead of the voices: sports or soap opera or an endless succession of commercials, I can't tell which. The set is as diminutive as the house itself – everything is miniature and yet there is hardly room to move: I seem to have entered an overstocked ark, bearing icons instead of animals. Cross-stitched antimacassars, that same reproduction of Khmelnitsky's *Triumphant Entrance into Kiev* which my parents have exiled to the garage, egg-sized busts of the great patriotic poets: Shevchenko, Ukrainka, Franko; brandy snifters crammed with painted easter eggs.

Mike gets up to greet me: he shakes my hand and won't let go until Annie gently disengages us, asking Mike to go to the kitchen and bring us something to drink. I have made it clear that I cannot stay for very long – I've only a week before I leave, there are still a hundred things to pack, and besides, my parents are expecting me for dinner. But the gift I've brought stays locked in my purse, for it is ginger ale, not whiskey Mike is offering. I'd forgotten that he doesn't drink anymore; the chocolates I chose are shaped like small casks filled with cognac and Cointreau and Courvoisier. And so I sit, hands clasped around my glass, my purse tucked well behind my feet, smiling and saying nothing as Mike and Annie, equally silent, smile back at me.

Mike and Annie. Their English names seem as familiar to them now as the shape of their hands or the shoes on their feet. But were I to call out *Miháhsh, Hányu*, who would answer me? I want us to talk to one another, I want to hear their stories, but we sit in a silence loud as any shouting. If only they could speak to me in their own language and not in an English that breaks in their mouths, falling in awkward pieces that I gather stealthily, so as not to embarrass them. If only I could feel at home in their language, if to speak it were not to feel a stump instead of a tongue in my mouth. And I feel before them the shame I knew as a child who could not understand more than a smattering of what my Ukrainian school teachers, who in Kiev and Lviv had been doctors and professors and who, in Toronto, were janitors and factory workers, called *móva réedna*, my true and native tongue.

As my mother says, I am going away for a long time, and who knows what may happen before I return. I have grown up under the eyes of these people. I have been told that they have had a hard life, and I, with my easy one, feel that edge of guilt which presses into everything that has to do with who and how I am. I am sitting here in Mike and Annie's living room because of a voyage made on a lucky hunch some forty years ago. Had my grandmother put off leaving Poland in 1936, had she stayed in the house where my mother was born, on land bought with the money my grandfather sent each month from Canada, then everything I am would be nothing. For my grandmother's house has disappeared, along with her village; the land she never sold belongs to a different country now, her only proof of ownership an envelope of brittle papers inscribed in a forbidden language: *moyèh pòleh* – my fields.

Mike and Annie have been lucky in a different sort of way. I know that they came to Canada after the war; that, like my Ukrainian school teachers, they were what we children called Dee-Pees, not knowing the grander terms on which they were with history: Displaced Persons. They survived the war, they made a new life for themselves – witness this house and all the belongings which make it look like a passport stamped on every page, with hardly a free space showing. Canada has been good to us, their silence seems to say – how can you leave, why are you going away? It's the same rebuke I seem to hear everywhere these days, and I counter it by talking too much and too fast. I don't know how much of what I say they understand – that I'm going by ship, that we dock first at Le Havre and then Tilbury, and that the boat goes on to Bremerhaven, Leningrad. I am studying English literature, I need to work with people in England, English is my mother tongue: English, not Ukrainian –.

There is silence then. I am reaching for my purse, signalling that it is time for me to go, when Mike begins to speak. He tells me that he and Annie went to England after the war.

'We be living in Leeds' – he pronounces it 'Lyeedz'. 'Five year. Annie, me, two both working in cloth factory. Five year until we coming to Toronto.' He is cradling the glass of ginger ale in his large, rough hands, but he does not drink.

'I be go to store one day. Five year I live in Lyeedz, and I be go to store, for buying' – he stops for a moment – '*bèelyee pahpèer.* "Paper white," I say, and shopkeeper, he look at me like I be dog or rat' – *rrrat*, he rolls his r's – '*Bèelyee pahpèer* behind him, on shelf, I point and he be shake his head, 'I no know what you want, go on, get out, *gerrrroutta heeerrrr.*'

Annie gets up from her chair and, touching Mike's hand, takes the glass away from him. Then she asks if I would like to see round the house. I nod my head too brightly, too quickly, as if to say, 'Yes, please, show me everything.' And so we go in procession, Annie letting her husband explain about the cupboards he has made for the kitchen, the new doors he has put onto the bedroom closet, the shower installed from a kit he picked up at the hardware. And that is the house: sitting room, kitchen, bathroom, bedroom. Doll-sized, and looking curiously exposed, the way in a doll's house the rooms are always missing a wall, so that you can look in and rearrange the furniture.

This is all there is of the house, but Annie says there's a surprise I must see. She takes my hand as if I were a child who must be protected from my own excitement; she opens a wooden door and leads me into a glassed-in porch filled with potted plants, their small green hands pressed against the windows, beseeching whatever light can fall through the narrow glass. Between the leaves I make out something blue, impossibly blue, like a billboard image of tropical seas. But as Annie pushes open the last door it is clear that what I took to be a mirage is really there: a swimming pool that takes up the whole of the cemented-over yard.

Were Annie and Mike to get into the pool together they would scarcely have room to turn. But I know without asking that no one swims here, any more than angels float suspended in the blue above us. A leaf from the neighbour's poplar drifts into the water: it floats, a golden coin, a small, eye-shaped fish, until Annie gets down on her knees and leans over the edge to pluck it out. As she folds the leaf into her pocket I realize that it is not the leaf but the pool's blue absolute that she is rescuing. I remember the child singing on the Bloor Street bus, her eyes the blue of ice melting, of streams running under snow; I remember Annie looking, longing. And for no reason, and because it seems, suddenly, needful, I find some words to say. I repeat what I remember of the child's song: *nach unten, nach unten.*

'*Nach unten geh'n.*'

It is Annie speaking now, not me. She pulls herself up from her knees: I can hear her bones speak: hoarse, straining for breath. *Nach unten geh'n* – that was how, she says, they asked permission of the guards to go down to use the latrines. 'In the camp,' she explains. 'Work camp, labour camp.' And that is all she says, either because she has run out of words, or because the words themselves have run out of any meaning they could give.

Mike has come to join us: Annie unfolds the leaf from her pocket and shows it to him; he nods his head. They do not touch one another, yet they seem joined in a way I had never recognized. Perhaps it is the narrowness of the cement strip on which they stand, or a trick of the light, like the illusion of blue with which the pool's painted floor infuses the water.

When I tell them it is late, now, that if I do not hurry I will miss my bus, they step apart. Annie asks Mike to walk me to the bus stop; I insist that it isn't necessary. Annie leads the way inside and then the two of them stand at the window, waving goodbye to me as I walk away from their house. I walk past the first and then the second stop; finally I flag down a cab and ride all the way downtown.

That night I phone my mother – for I have not gone home to dinner, I have met with friends and spent the evening taking leave. When I phone it is nearly midnight, but my mother goes to bed late, and always needs to talk, she says, before she can fall asleep. I say I have seen Annie and Mike in their new house. It is she who mentions the swimming pool, saying how crazy it is for them to have taken on a burden like that; how, with their love of gardening, they ought to have bought a house with a bit of land attached. My mother points out how dangerous it is for two people who have never learned to swim to have a pool in their backyard. Supposing a small child hopped the fence and fell in and needed rescuing? They could be sued, stripped of everything they own. And then she says something that shocks me, though of course I might have expected it. 'Annie's my age, you know.'

After I hang up I think of everything I didn't tell her: that I have been told a story about a shopkeeper in Leeds, and have discovered the one phrase in German that Annie can, or will remember. And I think of that curious expression on Annie's face, half longing, half delight, when she smiled at the child singing in the Bloor Street bus, and knelt to look into the clear and perfect eyes of the water.

I am far away now, from Annie's and my parents' houses; from the country in which I was born and the country I have known only through other people's memories and stories. Living so far away, I have gone to books and films and photographs to find out things that I could never ask of anyone at home, that no one could ever have told me, no matter how much they knew.

In one of the books which I have read since leaving home, I learned of how, after the Nazi occupation of Ukraine, many of that country's people were shipped to Germany: slave labour for camps and farms and factories. It often happened, the book said, that doctors would round up the young women before they were boarded onto the trains and, as if they were so many sturdy glass beakers, would sterilize them, to ensure the right kind of productive capacity and, more importantly, the purity of their future owner's race. I believe that this is what happened to Annie – I believe this because, of course, I could never ask her, and because I saw her once on the Bloor Street bus, looking longingly at a small German child as she may have looked through barbed-wire fences at the children who lived in the town beside the labour camp: as beings not so much apart as immune. Immune just as angels, with all the buoyancy of their beauty, are immune from dirt and suffering and death.

My mother has stopped mentioning Mike and Annie in her letters, and I have never inquired after them, as if the act of asking, directly, whether they are still alive, would make their deaths a certainty. But now and again, on that blurred, shifting border between sleep and waking, I have caught a glimpse of Annie. She is not, as I have so often seen her, bent over the earth of her garden. She no longer feels the need to grow flowers and fruit, to fill glass jars with beets and cucumbers and peaches. Instead, she is walking down into the blue, painted waters of her swimming pool, stretching out and gently floating, her face tilted up to the night. There are lights like fallen stars, shining from the bottom of the water: they show the body of a young girl, bathed clean of all stains and wounds, of all loss and longing. She is singing to herself, though I can't make out the words; in the cool, blue water she is singing.

Troglodytes

SUSAN SCHMIDT

Lizzie was a true yellow rose of Texas who still said words like 'ya'll' when she didn't catch herself first. 'Ya'll 're just puttin' me on, right?' she'd say, then correct herself quickly with 'I mean, you're just kidding me, aren't you?' She'd slip and use the word 'where' instead of the phrase 'so that'. 'I always listen to the Eagles where I won't get homesick,' she'd say. 'Just let me finish cuttin' up these onions where I can put them in the tuna salad.' She practised saying 'wash' over and over again, listening to the sound to make sure she wasn't saying 'warsh.' She concentrated on aspirating her ts. She worked on her diphthongs and spoke to herself in the mirror each morning to see if her nose moved. If her nose moved she knew she was talking too nasally.

Now that she'd moved here she never knew where she was any more because the sun arced on the horizon instead of directly overhead like it should. The streets curled and wandered instead of going straight in a grid. When people gave directions they never used the word 'blocks' but instead said things like 'three streets along'. As a result, Lizzie felt she was at the mercy of strangers and, for once, knew how Blanche Dubois felt in *A Streetcar Named Desire*.

But the strangers turned out to be *really* strange. Like they'd originally been creatures with shells and had somehow evolved over the eons so that now the actual shells had become invisible, but they didn't know it. It always took her a while each day to remember this fact; that people weren't going to make eye contact with her or speak to her when she walked down the street. After passing a few people she'd remember not to look in their faces any more, but straight ahead as if going towards God.

But neither God nor the mercy of strangers had been much help when he'd kicked her out.

When he'd kicked her out he hadn't been friendly about it. Actually, uncouth was the word for it, he'd been downright uncouth. Over the years she'd experienced her share of emotional retardees, played Wendy to a few Peter Pans and watched a couple of angry young men grow old overnight, but in all her sweet days she'd never seen the lights go out quite as dark and fast as the way he made them.

She'd met him in Austin at the El Azteca Café. She'd been gorging herself on her weekly dose of cheese enchiladas with red chillis and sour cream when he'd come in and sat down at the booth next to where she and her friend Carlene were seated. They heard him talking to the waitress. British, they'd mouthed to each other. An English accent. Everything about him looked foreign and exciting, like some kind of rock star. His hair was spiked on top, cut in a way you never saw in Austin, a foreign, sexy way like David Bowie's in the early eighties or something, and he wore a faded green denim vest over a shirt that looked western, but not on him. Eventually, as if on a dare from Carlene, she leaned over and said, 'You from England?' and smiled her shit-eating grin. One thing led to another and she'd found herself showing him around, taking him to Bad Frank's for a few beers, making out with him on a blanket by the lake, getting chigger bites all over her back as a result.

It had been what you might call a whirlwind romance, a veritable tornado of love coming out of nowhere, picking them up and depositing them on the shores of what-do-we-do-now? As it turned out, he wanted a green card so he could work in the States so, feeling like destiny had reached out of nowhere and struck her between the eyes, she married him. But six months later he got depressed and homesick, so they sold all her things and, on the money they got, split for England. 'For richer or poorer' she piously quoted to herself from her marriage vows whenever she had second thoughts about using her money to get them over here. She wasn't raised a Southern Baptist for nothing.

Then one day, seven or eight months after they'd settled in London, when she came home from working her evening cleaning shift at Debenham's, she walked over to him as he stood at the kitchen sink and put her arms around his waist to give him a hug. He pulled away and moved over to the fridge. He took out her jar of pickled okra and put it in a Safeway bag. He took the stack of frozen tortillas out of the freezer and her package of Oreos, a package of pinto beans and the bag of cornmeal out of the cabinet and put them in the bag. He added the jar of salsa but, she noticed, he left out the bottle of tequila.

'This should get you started,' he said.

'Started?'

'In your new place.'

'What new place?'

'The one you find without me in it.'

It had taken two weeks of looking in the classifieds and going to various houses to check out the rooms before she'd managed to find a place. In the meantime he disappeared, giving no further explanation. He'd come back to the flat when she was at work and leave notes like, 'The phone bill arrived. Your part is £57. Please do not make any more foreign phone calls before you move.'

* * *

Fred had spent the last five years in Paris working with André Jourdain who had been a star pupil and devotee of the corporal mime god, Etienne Decroux. Fred had learned to control every muscle of his body, every bone, being able to demonstrate at the drop of a hat his ability to make his body behave like a puppet on the strings of his mind. But André suddenly moved to Quebec, his students dispersed, and Fred, tired of Europe but not feeling inclined or ready to go back home to Minneapolis, decided to wander over to London.

At first he'd tried busking in Covent Garden. But people looked at him like he was a creature from a Cronenberg horror film. These audiences wanted their mimes to have white faces, spider-drawn eyes and teardrops on their cheeks. They wanted to see walls created with white gloved hands. When he started moving the various parts of his body to demonstrate his control, they at least expected it to lead into some kind of break-dancing routine. They were not in the least entertained.

He heard about the room in the flat in Archway from a sign that was posted in the cappuccino bar on Neal Street where he'd got a job waiting tables. The guy who was advertising the room was an art student, and he was moving in with his girlfriend. Fred agreed to take the room immediately and asked the student if he might be able to occupy right away. He spent three nights sleeping on the kitchen floor, waking to portraits in oil of people, friends of the artist supposedly, whom he hoped he'd never have to meet. The student finally moved out and took his paintings. Thankfully, he didn't introduce Fred to any of his friends.

As it turned out, the woman who had shared the flat with the artist/student decided to move out a week after the student did. She'd broken up with her boyfriend, played a Jane's Addiction tape over and over (it had been 'their' record), and the only times Fred ever saw her were when she'd come into the kitchen to make herself another cup of Morning Surprise tea. When she left she took the kettle, the Moulinex blender/coffee grinder, the television set and the tape deck. Luckily, she also took her Jane's Addiction tape.

'I'm afraid we're a little lacking in the finer comforts of life,' he apologized to Lizzie about the absence of appliances as he showed her around the flat. He noticed she didn't say much, that the bottom of her eyes had red semi-circles.

'I suppose you don't allow smokers?' she said defeatedly as though she were waiting to be rejected.

'Only if they smoke something stronger than these Light Silk Cuts.' He reached over to where his jacket hung on a peg in the hallway and lifted his pack of cigarettes out. He took one, then offered one to her. She smiled gratefully.

'I have to get up real early every morning to clean at Debenham's, then I have to go back at night.' She said this as if it were a factor even more damning than the smoking.

'You work at Debenham's?'

'I clean there. Five mornings and evenings a week. They have a different staff at the weekend.'

'Wow! Does that mean you could maybe pick up a few things, you know, pinch the occasional trash bag, I mean bin liner as they call it here . . . you know, the random cleaning product? Those things add up you know. With me bringing home the occasional scrap from the coffee bar, we could cut corners no end.'

'So this old man's at another window in the post office and he's yelling "I can't hear a bloody word you're saying," and the guy on the other side of the window says something else and all the other postal clerks on the inside laugh and all the people in my queue start shifting their feet and giving each other these amused little looks. It goes on like this the whole time I'm in the queue and the old man's getting more and more upset. So, I finally get my stamps and, since no one else is doing anything, and since the post office clerks are just shaking their heads and mumbling to themselves behind their glass, I go over to the old man and I ask if I can help him.

"What?" he snaps at me. He's real mad by now.

"Can I help at all?" I say.

"What?" he yells louder. "I can't hear a bloody word you're saying." He turned back to the guy at the window and started in on him again, so I just left. But everybody stared at me as I walked out the door.'

'That'll teach you,' Fred said, lighting a cigarette as they strolled along the South Bank of the river and crossed Waterloo Bridge. 'Maybe now you'll learn not to try to be so helpful. People don't like that here. It makes them think you think they're bad by not offering to help too. They feel guilty and confused, which of course they are, but they don't like being made to feel that way. They like to go about their lives thinking that God has a BBC accent and everything is "perfect really, thank you".'

Lizzie and Fred had arranged to meet after they each got off work. After several months of coming home each night, tired and drained, they'd grown bored with Scrabble, frustrated in their attempts to get a few answers to the *Guardian* crossword, and they'd taken to bringing books home from the library and reading to each other. Last week Lizzie had read Fred a Tony Hillerman thriller, but this week, for some ungodly reason Fred had chosen Plato. Out of all the books in all the world he'd brought home a collection of Plato's works and proceeded to read the one about the man in the cave. It was OK really, not exactly what she enjoyed listening to the most, but interesting in a rather strange way. It was about this guy who'd been in a cave for a really long time. Then, one day, this other guy comes along and leads him out. The man who's lived in the cave all this time can't believe what he sees around him and it blows his mind. It was an allegory, Fred explained, because it displayed in story-form the idea that each person is trapped inside his or her own little reality, own little cave-of-a-reality. It set Lizzie to thinking about things and the more she thought, the more disturbed she became. It seemed that she and Fred were getting more and more cave-like as the days went by so she finally suggested they needed to get out for a change. See what was out there, for god's sake. She'd been in London for almost a year and had been to Big Ben and the Houses of Parliament twice and that was about it.

They continued along the river and as they walked towards the Embankment tube station they were approached by more and more people asking for spare change. Others sat on the kerb, their hands permanently outstretched as though frozen in their stance of begging. One with a dog at his side, asked for money for dog food. An old lady sitting next to a trolley full of rags and odds and ends, said something totally indecipherable. As they approached the entry to the station a young woman with a small child sitting in a push-cart thrust her hand out in front of Lizzie.

'Spare some change for the baby?' she asked. Her eyes were glazed and her face was rife with red spots. The little boy's nose was running and he looked half asleep. Lizzie couldn't help thinking it wasn't just because it was his bedtime, but that he was suffering from malnutrition. She reached in the pocket of her jacket, pulled out her purse, and gave the woman a fifty-pence piece. The woman didn't thank her but quickly turned towards another passer-by and repeated her plea.

'They share the kid, you know,' Fred said as they slipped their tickets into the slots to enter the turnstile of the tube.

'What?'

'Those women,' he continued, 'I've heard they have shifts. One of them has a kid you see, and a bunch of them trade off. Each one takes him for a few hours to beg with. They get better money that way.'

'But that's horrible!' Lizzie said, outraged. 'What about the little boy?'

'Well, it's not as though they can put him in any kind of child care, can they?' They were silent for a few minutes as they made their way towards the platform. Once there they sat down and stared at the advertisement that was plastered on the wall across from them. It was a tourist advert, one that proclaimed the glories of vacationing in the Caribbean. Another one, next to it, promoted the benefits of a private health care scheme.

'Well, what would you do then?' Fred asked, 'if you had a kid and no money, no husband and no place to live, no job, no skills, a major recession going on . . .'

Lizzie thought for a moment. 'Well, for one thing, I'd get outta here.'

'Yeah, right. Where?'

'Home. I'd go home.'

'You mean the States, right? They've got homeless people in the States too, you know. Lots of them from what I hear. But, anyway, they don't have that option, they're British.' Fred didn't look at her as the train came in and they got on. They rode in silence for a while.

'But why don't they go home, back to where they came from?' she asked as though the conversation had been going on the whole time.

Fred shot her an exasperated look. 'Talk about The Allegory of the Cave! Where've you been?' He looked around helplessly, searching for where to start, what explanation to throw at her first. She wasn't stupid, but it seemed to him she suffered from terminal greenness and he couldn't imagine how she'd managed to survive and live in this city for almost a year and not know more than this. His irritation was assuaged by a sudden conclusion.

'Is it because you're from Texas, is that it? That must be it. Texans think there's always an easy answer.'

'What do you know about Texans?' she became defensive, then she caught herself and thought about it. Maybe that *was* the reason. At home whenever times had got rough in the past, you just went out and did something else. Even before she'd left, with the recession going on and people getting fired and things costing so much more, she'd still been able to find a way to make ends meet. Maybe it was different here. Maybe there weren't as many choices. Her mind swirled in trying to figure it out.

'Well, look, I may not know much about Texans,' Fred conceded, 'but you've got to stop putting such easy answers on things. There's just too much you don't know about to be taken into consideration.'

It wasn't exactly Fred's words that did it, it was everything. Thoughts, sensations and the night's revelations swirled together and crystallized themselves into a tiny pinpoint of realization. It didn't take long. In fact, by the time they'd reached Archway, exited the tube and started walking down the hill towards their flat, Lizzie had decided. She felt her steps come down firmly on the pavement, felt her shoulders actually relax for the first time in days as she looked up at the hazy night sky. Mercury could just barely be seen and the moon was almost full.

'Well, they may not be able to, but I can,' she said to him as though he'd been in on the conversation going on inside her mind.

'They may not be able to what, but you can?' His mind boggled.

'Go home!' She stopped and spread her arms out as if to welcome the air. He looked at her and smiled.

'That was quick. But, in a way, it took you long enough.'

She looked at him and wondered what he meant.

'I mean, it didn't take you long to make up your mind once you started thinking about it. But what I wonder is why it took you so long to think about it in the first place?'

They continued walking and she thought about what he'd said.

'Patty Hearst Syndrome,' she said, once again out of the blue.

'What?'

'I suffered from the Patty Hearst Syndrome. You know, captured and brainwashed into thinking that this was who I was, that destiny had led me to this? That's why it took me so long to see I needed to go home.'

Fred laughed as they entered the flat. 'Well, at least Patty Hearst had a few bucks behind her to get her out of *her* mess. How're you going to handle it?' They both looked around the sitting room of the flat. The sofa was littered with yesterday's *Guardian* and the Scrabble game sat at the edge of it. In the kitchen a single pan, unwashed since supper, sat on the cooker and a few dishes were stacked in the kitchen sink. It was the first time Lizzie had really looked at her situation and what she saw wasn't very comforting. She went over to the sofa and collapsed into it. Suddenly everything looked crushed and hopeless. Fred watched as she took it all in. She was beyond green. She was the first primordial speck of algae to appear upon the surface of the earth. He went over and sat down on the sofa next to her. Unable to fathom what the hell she'd occupied her mind with over the last months, *ever* for that matter, he heaved a sigh.

'Well, I guess what you have to do first is find out how much it costs to get back.' He looked over at her and, considering her track-record so far, wondered if she'd even be able to do that. 'There's this student place near work where they sell cheap tickets. Maybe you could go there and check it out.'

She looked at him, the daze on her face was still there, but with a new concern breaking through it.

'What about you?'

'Me?' He rolled his eyes up into his head and rubbed his hands through his hair. 'Oh god, me.' He reached into his jacket and pulled out a cigarette, lit it. 'Let's just not talk about me for now, OK? I mean, it's bad enough we have to talk about you.'

'But why don't you go home too?'

He inhaled a drag off the cigarette and let the smoke out slowly. He looked around the room, at the cracks coming down one of the walls, the ratty brown carpet, the peeling paint on the radiator. 'Let's just say I like it here,' he finally uttered, an ironic smile barely showing itself beneath the surface of his face. 'So many places to go, people to see, things to do.' He looked over at her and laughed at her dismayed expression. 'OK. Well then, maybe let's just say that I've always thrived on perversity.'

'Perversity?'

He saw that she had no way of understanding where he was coming from. 'Look,' he gave in, 'I'm not ready, that's all. Besides, there's nothing drawing me back. I left to go to Paris *for* something. But in this case, destiny doesn't call me, as you might put it.' He reached over and tousled her hair. 'Let's just focus on getting you back on the ranch, shall we?'

It was just before dark when they entered his flat. Lizzie had promised herself that she would not take stock of any signs of another woman's clothing or possessions. She would not grow nostalgic and morose if she saw his green denim vest hanging on the peg just inside the door, but would go straight to the task at hand. But, as it turned out, the signs were overwhelming, assaulting her as soon as they stepped through the door. There, on the other peg next to his vest, was a lady's cashmere coat and, on entering further into the room, she saw the vase of flowers, a new Habitat rug on the floor, and a tidiness about the place which he could never have managed. As she stood there looking around, Fred hurried over to the television, unplugged it and started coiling up the cord.

'What are you doing, for Christ's sake!' Fred hissed at her. 'We're not here for dinner, we're here to rip the bastard off, right?'

'Bastard!' she said, not simply repeating Fred's word, just saying it.

'Well, yeah, right, sure, come on then, we all know he's a bastard, nothing else is new, let's get the fuck out!' He went over to the stereo system and unplugged the cord from the power point. 'Here, you carry this, it's lighter.' She stood there, mesmerized by anger and frustration.

'He used all my money and . . .'

Fred walked over to her and grabbed her shoulders. 'Look, you're not Scarlett O'Hara and he's not the Yankees. You're here to get back your investment. And I'm not about to get caught stealing and thrown in an English jail and be buggered by a bunch of guys who all look like Oliver Reed and talk like Arthur Scargill on methadone. Now come on!' He put the stereo in her arms, picked up the television, and headed towards the door.

'Just a minute,' she said, and put the stereo down. She quickly headed for the bedroom and, without stopping to look around, opened the door of the clothes cupboard. Ignoring the dresses and other items of women's clothing which now hung where hers used to hang, she pulled out his shirts, his pair of black jeans, and every other thing that looked like his, slung them over her arm and headed back to the front room. Then she picked up the stereo and followed Fred out the door, not looking back.

She had managed to cram everything into just two suitcases and two carry-on bags. She had bought ten packages of Polos and a half dozen Bournvilles for the flight over, since she'd decided to give up smoking. Fred had announced that he was treating her to a mini-cab and was coming along for the ride.

On Friday, Fred had come home with three hundred pounds and a cassette recorder/radio ghetto blaster. He said the guy he'd sold the stuff to only had that much money but had thrown in the ghetto blaster as a sweetener. She'd been hoping for £350, but when she saw Fred's face light up as he turned the radio on and started playing with the dial, she realized it was only fair that he get something out of the deal. Besides, she liked thinking that she could remember him this way, with something to do besides play Scrabble or do crosswords with his next flat-mate.

As planned, they got out of the mini-cab at the station where they'd seen all the homeless people. Fred carried the heavy suitcases and Lizzie her carry-on bags. As they headed towards the beggars Lizzie motioned to Fred.

'Wait here, OK?' Fred smiled at her as he put down the suitcases, leaned against the wall of a building and looked at his watch. They'd timed it just right. After she did her thing they'd have just enough time to hail another taxi and make it to the airport.

'If you're not back in ten minutes I'll see you in the next life, OK?' he said as they exchanged grins.

As Lizzie walked close to the overpass where a cardboard city was set up, the street people seemed to come out of the woodwork. She soon saw the old lady with the trolley and the young woman, only a different one this time, with the little boy in the push-cart. Their hands reached out as if under water, their mouths bubbling words that couldn't make it to the surface. She started reaching into the bag.

She gave the old lady his brown and black cowboy shirt and the man with the dog his black jeans. She started at one side of the tunnel where the caves of cardboard started, then circled back on the other side when she came to the end. She pulled out his red football jersey, his white shirt for dressing up, the turquoise corduroy (the one which had always made his eyes look like he wore coloured contacts), the blue and black lumberjack shirt, the loose Mexican pullover. She didn't look at their faces, didn't listen for responses. She knew they'd rather have money, beer, something else. But she couldn't give them anything else. She only had this.

The Dream Shop

ROMESH GUNESEKERA

On Sundays, when I am at home, I like to go down to Anand's shop for the paper. He is good for a chat and keeps me in touch. This morning when I got there I found it had changed.

The shop had large new aluminium-frame windows and a new tough glass door. Against one wall a row of Sunday papers displayed the full diversity of English weekend reading. There were a couple of men and a gang of three kids milling around the counter choosing sweets. I was glad to see the place so busy: business seemed to have picked up. I felt overwhelmed by this sea of newsprint and quickly grabbed the thinnest paper I could reach and went to the counter, but Anand was not there. Instead a short young blond man punched the till. I handed over my money and asked him about Anand.

'He's gone! Didn't you know?'

I had an awful feeling that Anand had died while I was away. 'What happened?'

'I think he moved to Ealing or some place.'

'Ealing?'

'Or some place. I dunno. He sold up. He's gone.' He handed me my change and turned to serve another customer.

I had never seen the shop so crowded. The back room had been done up. Anand used to sell a few odd household items in that room: tissues, toothpaste, toilet paper. For bad planners he could offer real salvation on Sundays. That had all been swept away. Instead there were plastic toys and ice-creams: a white refrigerator gleamed in the corner.

It must have been about two years ago that I first discovered Anand's place. I sensed a *newness* like the smell of fresh paint in the centre of a row of grey buildings on Park Road.

In those early months Anand was always so perfectly dressed. He was in his late thirties and groomed like an accountant. His round shoulders, his calm hands, and the smooth almost aloof face gave him an air of deep seriousness. But on my very first visit he opened a simple conversation with me which was to carry on week after week in a seemingly unending exchange of brief quiet words.

'You know, we can deliver newspapers now,' he said, peering through an elegant pair of thin metal spectacles. 'You live in the area?'

I said I did.

He pulled a large red ledger from the shelf behind him and opened it carefully. 'What name shall I put down? It is only 5p.'

I gave my name and started on the address, but then changed my mind. 'No, never mind. I like the walk.'

He shrugged, 'Ok.'

It didn't seem right just to go, so I studied the confectionery.

'You are from Ceylon, isn't it? Sri Lanka?' he asked, rolling a pen between his fingers like a doctor.

I nodded, 'Yes, are you?' Suddenly he looked so familiar.

'No. I only thought so from the name. I had a friend from Sri Lanka. The name was like yours, same sound.'

'Are you from here then?' I asked, fumbling.

'No. East Africa. We had to leave.' He spoke softly, spacing the words; counting syllables.

I wondered where in East Africa, Uganda? But he didn't volunteer any more information and I didn't want to probe. Instead I asked about the shop.

He took a deep breath as if about to dive. 'We thought we will try the shop here. It's a good building. There is a flat upstairs.' He rocked on his stool. 'It is a start.'

Someone walked in and I thought I should leave. I said 'Good luck!' and saw his solemn face shift towards a smile.

As the weeks passed we talked more and more. One day he asked, 'Are you going to Sri Lanka this year?' I said it was too expensive to go, and there were troubles there. He nodded thoughtfully. Our relationship had developed into a kind of undeclared friendship. I looked forward to going down for the paper; if I was away, or unable to go, I would feel an absurd sense of loss. At the shop I would hang around as long as it took for the place to empty so that we could talk more privately. Towards the end of the summer I asked him whether he was happy with the way things were going.

'It's all right.'

And the family?

'They are OK. But you see, we are on our own here. Not many relatives.'

I asked where they were. In India?

'India? No, only my wife's people. My family is all over. I mean,' he smiled, 'all over the *place*. But here in London only one uncle.'

I urged him on; the streets were empty, nobody was coming in.

'It is difficult.' His mouth turned down at the corners in mock despair. 'You see, we do not agree. We should have gone into partnership. He has a shop in Ealing . . .' Anand

shook his head, 'but he is old and very stubborn. I wanted
to go into the audio-video business. I have the training – the
technical training – but capital is the problem. You need a
lot. And he would not agree. So we had to try something
else. This place. A traditional small shop.' He shrugged his
big round shoulders like a porpoise shedding the sea. 'If it
works, then maybe we can go into video. That is my dream.
A high-tech shop . . .'

'In Park Road?'

He looked bemused.

Then last winter my work disrupted everything. I had to
travel up and down the country and rarely had a weekend at
home. Only once, back in February, did I manage to get to
Anand's. The inside of the shop seemed dark as though all
the lights had been dimmed, the bulbs replaced by low-
watt bulbs. It was cold. I was shocked to find Anand
unshaven and bleary-eyed; his normally crisp white shirt
was grimy. He was staring at the till. I looked down at the
newspapers. The stacks were all uneven: some nearly sold
out, others beached in huge oversubscribed heaps. I tried
not to notice the changes and asked Anand, as I usually do,
'How are things?'

He shook his head as if trying to get water out of his ear.
'Difficult. In this country it is so difficult. People . . .'

'Why? What has happened?'

'Nothing,' he mumbled. 'You can't blame them, I suppose. It's the weather. Nobody wants to go out in this
wretched weather.' He nodded at the bit of dirty sky visible
out of the window. 'How can you sell anything?' He looked
at me gloomily.

The bell on the door jangled and two small boys stamped
in with a cloud of cold air. They came up to the counter and
asked for two chocolate bars. When they left Anand turned

to me. 'Those two are OK, but some of these kids are impossible.' He rubbed his swollen cheeks.

I asked him what he meant.

'They come and just take what they want and run.'

'You mean steal?'

'Steal? Yes. They come and take and run off. What can I do? I can't leave the shop and run after them, somebody else will come and take everything.'

Could he not keep them out, I asked.

'I don't let the stealers in. I shoo them like cats. But then there are others. Always new ones. They don't take much – toffees, crisps – but, you know, it's all money going.' He looked despondent. 'This time of year is no good . . . But how about with you? Have you been to your Sri Lanka?'

I said I hadn't, just been out of town on business.

'Next winter I think we will go to India. Somehow sell something and go.'

I asked him whereabouts.

'Gujerat. My wife's people.' He stared out of the window. 'There is no one else to go to.'

'And how about your uncle?'

He sighed. 'He is very sick, very sick. My wife has to look after him also. This is our life.' He looked to me for agreement.

That was two months ago.

And now he has gone to Ealing! I try to picture him, dressed in his black suit, unloading brand-new video cartons from the back of a big van.

About the Authors

Roberta Allen is the author of *The Traveling Woman* and *The Daughter*, both collections of stories, and *Amazon Dream*, a travel memoir. She is also a visual artist who has exhibited around the world. She lives in New York.

Joe Ambrose has co-written *Man From Nowhere; Storming the Citadels of Enlightenment with William Burroughs and Brion Gysin*. He is one of the editors of *Nagual Time*, a quarterly arts magazine. He lives in London where he manages a rock group, The Baby Snakes.

Brooke Auchincloss-Foreman was born in Manhattan and moved to Britain in 1981. She works as an art director and computer illustrator and lives in London.

Leena Dhingra was born in India and came to Europe following the Partition of India in 1977. Her publications include *Amritvela*, a novel. She lives in London.

Romesh Gunesekera was born in Sri Lanka and now lives in London. His book of stories *Monkfish Moon* was published by Granta Books in 1992. His next book, a novel, is due to be published later this year.

Kirsty Gunn has had stories published in Faber's *Introductions II*, *Slow Dancer* magazine and has recently had a story broadcast on Radio 4. She lives in London.

Roy Heath was born in Guyana and is the author of *The Murderer*, *Orealla* and *Shadows Round the Moon*, his autobiography. He lives in London.

Aamer Hussein was born in 1955 in Sind, Pakistan. He now lives in London, where he writes, lectures and translates. His stories and essays have been published in China, the USA, Indonesia, India, Pakistan and the Philippines.

Janice Kulyk Keefer is the author of *Constellations, The Paris-Napoli Express, Traveling Ladies,* and *Rest Harrow.* Born in Toronto, she is currently Professor of English at the University of Guelph in Ontario, Canada.

Hooman Majd was born in Tehran, Iran in 1957 and educated at St Paul's and George Washington University in the USA. As the son of a diplomat, he lived around the world including Tunisia, India, England and the United States. After the Islamic Revolution of 1979, he settled in Los Angeles. Currently he lives in New York, where he is vice-president of A&R for Polydor Records, and is working on his first novel.

Jaime Manrique is the author of *Latin Moon in Manhattan* and his epic poem 'Christopher Columbus on his Deathbed' is forthcoming. He writes in both English and Spanish and teaches at the New School for Social Research in New York, where he lives.

During the 1960s, '70s and '80s, **Susan Moncur** was at the top of the modelling profession. Photographed by Sarah Moon, Helmut Newton and David Bailey, among others, her reign at the top lasted fifteen years, until her 'retirement' at the age of thirty-four. She has since begun a career as a writer and a journalist, and her first book, *They Still Shoot Models My Age*, was published by Serpent's Tail in 1991. An American by birth, she has lived in Paris since 1970.

Since coming to England from Canada in 1982 **Kate Pullinger** has written *Tiny Lies, When the Monster Dies,* and *Where Does Kissing End?* She lives in London.

John Saul lives in Hamburg, Germany, where he works for Greenpeace. He has had some thirty stories published in magazines and in anthologies. His novel *Heron and Quin* was published by Aidan Ellis in 1990.

Susan Schmidt was born in Texas and has lived in California and New Mexico. She has published poetry, managed a contemporary theatre company and produced jazz concerts. Her novel, *Winging It*, was published in 1991. She emigrated from America to Britain in 1986 and now lives in London.

Josef Skvorecky became one of Czechoslovakia's most popular writers after his first novel *The Cowards* was banned by the communist regime. He is the author of, amongst others, *The Bass Saxophone*, *The Engineer of Human Souls*, *Dvořák in Love* and *The Miracle Game*. He now lives in Toronto, Canada, where he emigrated in 1968.

Lynne Tillman was born in New York City, where she still lives. She is the co-director and writer for the feature film *Committed*, and author of three novels, *Haunted Houses*, *Motion Sickness* and *Cast in Doubt* and a collection of stories, *Absence Makes the Heart*.

Audrey Thomas is the author of, amongst others, *The Wild Blue Yonder* and *Graven Images*, her twelfth novel. She also writes for radio and her work has been broadcast on BBC radio. Born in New York State, she now lives in British Columbia, Canada.

Janette Turner Hospital is the author of, amongst others, *The Ivory Swing*, *The Tiger in the Tiger Pit*, *Borderline*, *Charades* and *The Last Magician*. An Australian who now lives in Canada, she spends half the year as Adjunct Professor of English at La Trobe University in Melbourne.

Founded in 1986, Serpent's Tail publishes the innovative and the challenging.

If you would like to receive a catalogue of our current publications please write to:

FREEPOST
Serpent's Tail
4 Blackstock Mews
LONDON N4 2BR

(No stamp necessary if your letter is posted in the United Kingdom.)